Magic & Midnight

Starry Hollow Witches, Book 16

Annabel Chase

Red Palm Press LLC

Copyright © 2022 by Annabel Chase

All rights reserved.

No part of this book may be reproduced in any form or by any electronic or mechanical means, including information storage and retrieval systems, without written permission from the author, except for the use of brief quotations in a book review.

❦ Created with Vellum

Chapter One

"If you walked any slower, we'd be going backwards," I said to the small Yorkshire terrier at my feet. Some people counted dog-walking as exercise. I counted it as moonwalking.

I looped the handle of the dog leash over the fencepost and crouched to inspect the herb garden outside Rose Cottage. The Yorkie didn't protest. He simply sank into the grass and closed his eyes. Prescott Peabody III, or PP3 as he was affectionately known, was too ancient to care about chasing butterflies or running riot through rows of mint, sage, and belladonna, which worked for me because Marley would murder me if anything happened to her precious plants on my watch. And the belladonna would murder PP3, which was one of the main reasons we set up a protective ward around the garden.

A strong breeze blew past me, whipping petals and seeds into the air. I cringed and hoped I wasn't responsible for that little snafu. I'd incited a change in the weather under stressful circumstances in the past, so it was possible. Then again, I wouldn't describe my current emotional status as stressed. If anything, life was finally beginning to work with me instead of against me. I was no longer a salmon swimming upstream, unless you counted my recent culinary efforts that resulted in condensed milk on the ceiling. Don't ask.

Lavender floated to the ground, coating the grass in a soft layer of purple. I tried to recall the plant's attributes. Marley seemed to know them all by heart, whereas I was still trying to remember which ones would kill me. It was hard to believe that once upon a time belladonna had been used by witches as a flying ointment. I was relieved that was no longer the case. I struggled with accurately measuring cups of flour for cookies. I didn't trust myself to measure the precise amount of belladonna to save me from certain death.

I pushed aside the negative thoughts of belladonna and tried to focus on a plant with more positive associations. Lavender would do. Never mind the association with elderly British women.

I pivoted to the dog. "Peace, harmony, tranquility, serenity, grace, and calmness. And, yes, I realize some of those are just synonyms."

There you go. My brain wasn't broken after all. Gold star for Ember.

I gazed at the remnants of lavender on the ground. It looked like a dusting of purple snow. Another fact popped into my head. Purple was the color associated with the crown chakra. Maybe a lavender snow angel would help me absorb its attributes by osmosis. Waste not, want not.

I dropped to my bottom and sprawled on my back, moving my arms and legs through the smooth flowers. I didn't care if I looked ridiculous to the universe.

"I'm connecting with my higher purpose," I told the sky.

Now that I'd made up with Aunt Hyacinth, I had energy to spend on other pursuits.

I stared at the sky and watched the clouds drift overhead. My muscles relaxed. The lavender seemed to be working. The world felt peaceful.

A flash of movement interrupted my spiritual awakening. At first glance I thought it was Bonkers, my daughter's familiar, until I realized this creature was the wrong color. I turned my head for a closer look. The creature sat atop a nearby fencepost and faced the garden.

"Hey, a flying squirrel."

PP3 opened one eye as though debating whether to lodge an objection to the critter's presence. In the end, he opted to return to his nap. The lavender seemed to have lulled him into a state of calm as well.

I observed the flying squirrel with interest. He had the biggest eyes I'd ever seen on a creature his size. We're talking cartoon quality.

"Hey there, Rocky. You're super cute, but don't touch these plants no matter what or I'll have to hire a vengeance demon to track you down. My daughter has worked too hard on this garden to let it fall prey to wildlife, no matter how adorable you are."

Although the ward seemed intact, one could never be too careful. Marley and I didn't have a lot of experience with protective wards. Every day was a work in progress. Kind of like my life in general.

I rolled onto my stomach to see two white leather boots at eye level. I bolted upright and dusted the lavender from my clothes.

"Lazy Sunday?" Marigold asked, smirking.

"How did you manage to sneak up on me in a pair of go-go boots? I should've heard the swinging sound of the

Sixties a mile away." I glared at the aging Yorkie. "Some watchdog you are."

PP3 seemed perfectly content to ignore the both of us.

"If you must know, I'm working on a project for a client," I lied.

She smirked. "In a bed of lavender? I'd love to know more about it."

"Sorry. Client confidentiality." I rose to my feet and ignored the unpleasant twinge in my lower back. I motioned to the boots. "What brings you to whiten my doorstep? Let me guess. You heard I'm back in Aunt Hyacinth's good graces and want to tutor me again."

"Something like that."

"No thanks. I'm a busy lady. Haven't you heard? I've got my own P.I. firm to run. Bills to pay. No time to improve my skills so that my aunt isn't embarrassed by me."

"This isn't about Hyacinth."

I regarded her. "Oh, you want to help so that *you're* not embarrassed by me? Even less of an incentive." I started toward the door.

"This is about Ivy's magic," Marigold blurted.

The mention of my powerful ancestor got my attention. I halted in my tracks and twisted to look at her. "What about it?" I could count on one hand the number of people that knew I possessed Ivy Rose's magic, or so I believed.

Marigold lowered her gaze. "I know you've...inherited some of it, or all of it. I don't know the details. I only know what I felt when we swapped bodies that day. The raw power." She shook her head. "I've been worried about you, Ember. It's incredibly powerful magic and you don't have the training or experience necessary to handle it."

Her tone sounded sincere. "Come inside and we'll talk."

Marigold joined me in the kitchen where I poured each

of us a glass of burstberry iced tea. We stared at each across the island.

"Do you swear this isn't a Hyacinth directive?" I asked. It wouldn't be the first time Marigold lied to me.

The Mistress of Psychic Skills held up her hands. "I swear. It's been gnawing at me. I know what happened to Ivy and I don't want to see that happen to you."

That made two of us. My ancestor was once a High Priestess of the Silver Moon coven whose magic packed a Hulk-like punch. The coven turned on her out of fear and Ivy ended up hiding her magic in her Book of Shadows before they stripped her of it. When I managed to unlock her Book of Shadows using her wand, I inadvertently absorbed the magic contained in the book.

"Tell me what you felt when we Freaky Friday'ed," I said.

Marigold arched an eyebrow. "That's a verb now?"

I shrugged. "Everything's a verb if you use it properly."

"When I inhabited your body, I sensed you were housing Ivy's magic," Marigold admitted.

"How?"

"Because I know you, Ember. What I felt in that moment wasn't you. The energy was like nothing I'd ever felt before." She shuddered. "And then I heard that you basically exploded a workshop single-handedly."

I drew my shoulders back. "You seem to forget I'm powerful in my own right. I've summoned thunderstorms complete with lightning bolts. I'm basically the witch version of Zeus—without the sexual predation, of course."

She sipped her iced tea. "I agree that's impressive, but it isn't the same as what I experienced."

I chewed my lip, debating how much information to divulge. Truth be told, I trusted Marigold and knew she had my best interest at heart, despite the sting of betrayal when she withdrew her services at my aunt's request. I understood she'd been placed in a difficult position. We all had.

I placed my palms flat on the counter. "Okay, cards on the table. Let's say, hypothetically, that I am the proud new owner of Ivy's magic. What would you do about it?"

"That's simple. Help you learn to use it properly so it doesn't hurt you or anyone else."

"Your expertise is in psychic skills and that only covers a fraction of Ivy's abilities. How do you expect to help me?"

Marigold swallowed a mouthful of iced tea. "I didn't say it's a perfect system. If you really want to pull out the big guns, then you should make an announcement at the next coven meeting. That'll get you the support you need. We have a witch or wizard for every skill. That's the beauty of being a member of a coven."

The thought of dozens of witches and wizards lining up to experience a piece of Ivy's power was unsettling, to say the least. I'd feel more like a show pony than a person.

"I don't need that level of support, Marigold. I'm fine. What happened in that workshop was self-preservation. I don't feel out of control."

Marigold gave me a wry smile. "I'm sure Ivy said the same thing at one point." She set the glass on the island. "I've kept this information to myself for your sake, Ember. When I tell you I'm only here to help you, I mean it."

I mulled over the offer. "What would this tutoring involve?"

"I've taken the liberty of drawing up a proposal." She withdrew a folded sheet of paper from her pocket and handed it to me. "It's only a rough idea. We can tweak it as needed."

I studied the contents of the paper. There were bold

and italicized letters and underlined terms. A schedule with progress targets. Marigold had clearly given this plenty of thought.

I glanced from the paper to Marigold. "Why would you do this for me?"

"I told you. I don't want to see anybody hurt if you have some sort of nuclear meltdown, nor do I want to see a repeat of the witch hunt that took place with Ivy. It was bad for the coven, as well as her."

I drummed my fingers against the side of my glass. "Are you sure you want to do this? If Aunt Hyacinth knows you're helping me, she still might hold a grudge. After all, I have the power she thought she deserved."

She cocked her head. "As long as I don't put your delicate truce at risk, I'm willing to take my chances with her."

"I'm taking my chances with her tonight. I've finally been invited back to Sunday dinner."

"That's a good start," Marigold said. "How do you feel about it?"

"Hungry." I patted my stomach. "I'm skipping lunch so I have plenty of room for dinner and dessert."

"A well-thought-out plan." She frowned. "Where is Marley?"

I rolled my eyes. "She has a new best friend at the academy. Suddenly every day revolves around Jinx's schedule. She's even skipping our first dinner back at Thornhold to eat with Jinx's family."

"Coven members, I presume."

I nodded. "The Green-Warts."

Marigold wrinkled her nose. "Yes, I've had the pleasure of playing golf with Twila on occasion."

"You golf?"

"I do many things that don't revolve around you, Ember."

"I bet you're ridiculously competitive." I didn't refer to her as the cheerleader-meets-drill sergeant for nothing.

"So is Twila, so we're evenly matched in that regard."

"You really think I should tell the coven about Ivy's magic?" I hated secrets and I'd been hoping to unload this one as soon as the time was right.

"I've heard whispers about your possession of Ivy's wand and books, so I think it's only a matter of time before everyone knows the full extent of the situation, but I'm also concerned that the knowledge will invite certain problems. You have to understand, Ivy Rose has an almost mythical status among some coven members. If they think you can somehow channel her…"

I scoffed. "I'm not a medium. I can't channel. It's only her magic." I omitted the part about the connection I felt to the former High Priestess. It made sense given our familial connection.

"If it were me, I'd hold off for now. Maybe once we feel comfortable with your level of control. Speaking of which —" Marigold slapped her hands on the counter. "What do you say? First tutoring session this week? I'll put you on the schedule right now."

"What do we tell people? Everybody knows my lessons stopped."

"You can tell them whatever you like. Now that you have your own business, you're brushing up on skills that you might use during investigations."

"Yes, astral projection comes in real handy during surveillance." I gulped down my iced tea. "Fine. I'll accept your offer of help." Mainly because Ivy's history terrified me. Marley was still young. She needed a mother who wasn't in danger of jumping off the magical deep end. "On one condition."

"And what's that?"

I inclined my head toward the floor. "You don't wear those boots."

"I don't understand what you have against these boots. They're vintage."

"So are parachute pants, but I'd object to those, too."

"Fine. No white boots." Marigold tapped the glass. "Good job with this. Just the right amount of tart."

"Are you talking about me or the iced tea?"

She pulled a face. "I'll show myself out."

Chapter Two

I arrived at Thornhold with my hair brushed and sort-of styled and an outfit that wasn't covered in lavender. I was sure my aunt would manage to find fault with my appearance anyway, but at least I'd made an effort.

Simon greeted me at the door. "Welcome back, Miss Ember. You're wanted in the study."

"The study? Am I early for dinner? I thought Florian said five-thirty."

Simon's mouth twitched. "I'm sure he did, miss."

I entered the study to find only Aunt Hyacinth and Florian. My aunt wore her trademark kaftan, this one with a porcupine design. Maybe I was skidding dangerously close to middle age, but this kaftan was actually kind of cute. Her white-blond hair was swept up in a chignon and secured with a golden comb.

I motioned to the desk. Instead of paperwork, there was a white candle at either end and a bowl of mixed herbs in the middle. "What's all this? Valentine's Day is months away."

"An effort to mend fences," Florian said. "Mother, I'd

like you to sit at this end of the desk and Ember, you sit at the other."

"Florian, this really isn't necessary," I said.

"Of course it is. You've let this conflict drag on long enough. It's affecting the whole family, not just the two of you."

Clearly Florian had been too wrapped up in his new relationship with Honey Avens-Beech to realize his mother and I had resolved our differences.

To my surprise, Aunt Hyacinth sat as directed. When I shot her a quizzical look, she winked.

I followed suit and sat at the opposite end of the desk from her. Florian used his wand to light the wicks.

"Wow, I can't remember the last time I saw you lift a wand," I observed.

"Anything for the cause," he said. "Now, I've taken the liberty of mixing a few herbs that should help with the conflict resolution."

"You mixed herbs?" Aunt Hyacinth asked. "With your own mortar and pestle?"

"Yes. Admittedly I needed Simon to unearth them for me because I had no idea where they were, but I made the concoction myself."

I looked sideways at him. "Was this Honey's idea?"

"I'm certain it was," my aunt said.

Florian's cheeks reddened. "Does it matter whose idea it was? The important part is that I'm the one executing the plan."

"All by yourself." I nodded my approval. "Florian's a big boy now."

"We hate to spoil your attempt at being proactive, but the truth is that Ember and I have reached an accord."

Florian glanced from his mother to me. "Seriously? I did all this for nothing?"

I waved a hand. "All what? Busted out two candles and a bowl of potpourri? You'd put more effort into seducing a random fairy from Elixir."

Florian straightened. "Those days are over. I'm with Honey now."

I leaned over to blow out the candle closest to me. "Not the point."

"We appreciate your efforts, truly, darling," Aunt Hyacinth said.

Florian snatched the bowl off the desk and clutched it to his chest. "I think I hear Linnea and the kids at the door."

I laughed. "Don't be like that. We really do appreciate what you tried to do."

The wizard met my gaze. "I want us to be a family again. I've spent time with Honey and Castor recently and it's made me realize how much I missed *us*. The whole Rose clan."

I resumed a standing position. "Well, you'll have us all together for dinner tonight except Marley."

"A shame," Aunt Hyacinth said. "But I think it's excellent news that she's bonding with a witch from a good family."

I smiled at her. "The Green-Warts have your stamp of approval?"

"I'd place them in the same tier as the Avens-Beech family," she said.

Only my aunt would categorize families by tiers.

Simon appeared in the doorway. "Everyone is in the dining room, madam."

"Thank you, Simon. If you could have my aperitif on the table..."

Magic & Midnight

"Already taken care of." He bowed and walked away.

The three of us walked to the dining room together and I saw the elation on Aster's face as we entered the room.

"Ember's here," Aspen announced, as though no one else could see me.

No one made a fuss over me—that wasn't the Rose way—but I felt the love and relief all around me as we settled in and enjoyed our appetizers. Aunt Hyacinth must've put some thought into the menu because bacon-wrapped scallops were one of my favorites.

"What would you think of going back to Yarrow?" Aunt Hyacinth asked as a platter of roast chicken floated to the table.

I fixed her with a hard look. "Just because we're on the bumpy road to Friendtown doesn't mean I'm going to debase myself with a ridiculous name."

She sniffed. "Because Ember is so much better?"

"No Yarrow. Not now. Not ever."

"And here I thought we were mending fences."

"Mending fences doesn't mean I do whatever you want. This relationship isn't a one-way street."

"You tell her, Jersey."

All heads swiveled to the doorway where Wyatt Nash stood. He wore jeans with a gaping hole in the knee and a blue-grey T-shirt with *In My Defense I Was Left Unsupervised* written in block letters.

Simon drew up behind the werewolf, panting heavily. "Apologies, madam. He was too fast for me."

"Me, too," Linnea quipped. "How do you think this one got here?" She inclined her head toward Bryn.

"Can we help you with something, Wyatt?" Aunt Hyacinth asked. She seemed remarkably calm considering her former son-in-law had interrupted her beloved Sunday dinner.

"Linnea said I could have dinner with the kids today. I went by the inn and nobody was home, so I tracked them here."

Linnea heaved a sigh. "Wyatt, you know perfectly well I would never agree to let you have them for dinner on a Sunday."

He scented the air. "Something smells good. What's on the menu tonight?"

I stared at my plate in an effort not to laugh. He'd put Hyacinth in an impossible position. The hostess in her wouldn't be able to refuse him an invitation to join us.

"Roast chicken," Hudson volunteered. "It's got that seasoning you like."

Wyatt rubbed his stomach. "I sure do remember that fondly."

"Would you like to join us?" my aunt asked through clenched teeth.

"Don't mind if I do." Wyatt wedged himself between Bryn and Linnea.

"I'll fetch an extra place setting and a chair," Simon said with a slight bow.

"I don't think we need the chair," Wyatt said. "Linnea doesn't mind sharing hers."

Linnea cut a glance over her shoulder. "And a chair, please, Simon. A wide one with the thickest arms you can find."

Wyatt rubbed his hands together as he examined the offerings on the table. "Boy, Sunday dinners are the best, aren't they?" He seemed to direct this question to Aspen and Ackley.

The twins regarded their uncle with trepidation.

"Where's the big guy? Doesn't he rate an invite to family dinners? I mean, I can relate."

"Rick is working." Linnea proceeded to stab her roast chicken multiple times with her fork.

Wyatt smirked. "You know that chicken's already dead, don't you?"

Linnea feigned surprise. "Oh, is this chicken? I was imagining something else."

Simon returned with a bulky chair. A place setting floated past him and landed in front of Wyatt on the table. Linnea and Bryn inched their chairs apart to make room, forcing Hudson closer to Aunt Hyacinth, the spot usually reserved for Marley.

Wyatt looked at me. "And what about my brother? Have you two reached the Sunday dinner phase of your relationship or are you taking it slow?" He stole a piece of meat off Linnea's plate and chewed. "He must not remember how good the food is here if he's taking it slow. Chef's kiss as usual, Hyacinth."

"This is my first Sunday dinner in ages," I said. "I don't expect an invitation to be extended to Granger, too."

"You two are serious, though, right?"

Leave it to Wyatt to immediately make things awkward.

Wyatt didn't wait for me to respond. He shifted his attention to Florian. "Speaking of serious, I saw you out with Honey Badger," Wyatt said, chewing with his mouth open. "Did you seal the deal yet?"

"Wyatt!" Linnea elbowed him in the ribs.

Laughing, Wyatt rubbed the injured area. "I mean did you get down on one knee? Get your mind out of the gutter, Linnea. There are children present."

"Honey and I are taking our time to get to know each

other," Florian replied. "And I'm making sure I don't do anything to screw it up."

"Well, she's not a Rose, so she has that going for her."

"Hey," Bryn objected. "I'm a Rose."

"Yeah, but you're more Nash than Rose," the werewolf said.

The fact that Linnea married a werewolf was bad enough, but the fact that both their children favored their werewolf side annoyed Aunt Hyacinth to no end. Wyatt seemed intent on pushing all the buttons tonight.

"If I could've controlled that outcome, I would have," my aunt said.

"Can't be helped, really. We wolves like to dominate." He pointed a fork at me. "You ought to remember that before you commit to any kids with my brother. Chances are they'll turn out like these two."

"There's nothing wrong with our children," Linnea insisted. "Now put food in your mouth and stop talking."

Wyatt made a show of shoveling more chicken into his mouth. "Why not do both? And here you thought I couldn't multi-task."

"Well, I'm having a challenging week," Aster said, clearly in an attempt to seize control of the uncomfortable conversation.

"What's the problem?" Florian asked.

She took a sip of wine and set down the crystal glass. "Supply chain issues are having a negative impact on Sidhe Shed." Aster had recently started her own company that manufactured and sold small outdoor buildings. In fact, my office for R&R Investigations was one of Aster's creations and it was perfect.

I savored my wine, happy to be back in a place where

expensive wine I couldn't afford was served. "What kind of issues?"

Aster ticked them off on her fingers. "Fabric for curtains. Cement. Breakfast cereal."

"Wait, what does breakfast cereal have to do with your business?" Linnea asked.

"Nothing, but the twins can't get their favorite brand and it's destroying our morning routine."

Sterling nodded in sympathy. "They're very particular."

"We like what we like," Aspen said matter-of-factly.

Wyatt offered a fist bump from across the table. "I'm right there with you, little buddy."

"You don't remember my name, do you?" Aspen lifted his chin slightly, challenging the werewolf.

"Sure I do. You're Aster's kid."

"That's not a name," Aspen said.

Ackley drummed his small fingers on the table. "We're waiting."

The twins stared at him with blank expressions.

Wyatt leaned back in his chair, acting aggrieved. "What is this—*The Shining*? Can't a guest eat in peace?" He fell silent and continued to scarf down his meal.

Linnea gave the boys an approving smile.

Despite Wyatt's interruption, it was good to be back in the Rose embrace. I was sure I left the house five pounds heavier, but it was worth it. With a full container of leftovers in tow, I arrived at the cottage to find Granger leaning against his patrol car in the driveway.

"And here I thought my night couldn't get any better." I greeted him with a light kiss on the lips.

"What time do you have to pick up Marley? I thought we might sneak in a little quality time."

"They're driving her home in an hour."

Grinning, he encircled my waist. "What could we possibly do between now and then?"

I kissed him again.

"How was your first dinner back?" he asked.

"Good. Did you eat? Simon sent me home with leftovers." I tapped the container squished between us.

"Not yet. Crime doesn't stop just because it's dinnertime."

On cue, his phone buzzed. Releasing me, he frowned at the screen. "And duty calls again. Care to go for a quick drive?"

"Sure. Where to?"

"Balefire Beach."

"In the dark? I guess that's romantic."

"You won't say that when you see the reason we're going there."

Well, that wasn't ominous or anything. "Can't you send Bolan or Pitt?"

"Bolan's already there. Pitt's away visiting a sick relative this week so we're short-staffed."

"Let me run this chicken inside and let PP3 out to pee."

By the time I finished my tasks, the sheriff was waiting in the car with the motor running. We arrived at the beach and I noticed a cluster of silhouettes gathered at the water's edge.

"Busy night at Balefire Beach," I remarked.

"Maybe there was a bonfire tonight."

I tripped on the sand and Granger caught my wrist before I faceplanted on the beach. I looked behind me for the culprit and noticed tire track indentations in the sand. "Since when are dune buggies allowed here?"

His gaze was still directed at the shoreline. "They're not. I'll have Bolan put up a new sign, not that I think the

Magic & Midnight

kids bother to read them." He cast a quick glance at me. "You don't happen to have your wand, do you?"

"No. Sorry."

He produced a pen light from his pocket and used it to illuminate the remainder of the walk.

As the scene came into focus, I saw that Bolan had set up a perimeter of tape. Instead of the usual bright yellow, however, this tape featured rainbows and sparkles. It was the body facedown on the sand that really grabbed my attention, though.

The man wore board shorts with no shirt. His feet were bare and covered in wet sand. I spotted a surfboard a few feet away from the body.

"Was it a shark attack?" one of the observers asked.

"Deputy said no sign of teeth marks," the woman beside him said.

Using his fingers in his mouth, the sheriff blew a shrill whistle. "Show's over, folks. I'm going to need everybody to clear the area."

"Do you think it was a siren attack?" the same observer asked. "Maybe she tried to lure him to the bottom of the ocean and he fought back."

"I only just got here, so I don't know what to think at this point," the sheriff said. "Deputy Bolan, would you be so kind as to escort the onlookers to another part of the beach and give us space?"

"No problem, Sheriff." The leprechaun set to work ushering the crowd away from the rainbow tape.

I stared at the body. "Any ID?"

"Don't need it," Granger said. "I know who he is. Zed Barnes. We call him the Midnight Surfer."

"Who surfs at night?"

"Someone who doesn't like to be around others. Zed

was somewhat of a hermit. He only surfed under the cover of darkness so he could avoid others."

I gazed at Zed's long, white hair tied in a ponytail. Maybe it was still the lavender talking but he looked peaceful—except for the patch of blood matted to his hair.

The sheriff sniffed the air. "There's more blood." He ambled over to inspect the surfboard. "It's here."

I craned my neck for a better view. "Somebody whacked him in the back of the head with his own surfboard?"

"Maybe, or could be that a wave toppled him and the surfboard hit him in the back of the head. They both washed to shore. His hair's still damp so he hasn't been out of the water too long."

Deputy Bolan returned to the crime scene. "I'll check the surfboard for prints unless you've already done it."

"Be my guest," the sheriff said.

"What's with the special tape?" I asked the leprechaun.

"I was in a hurry to get here. I opened the drawer and grabbed the roll on top, but it turned out to be my husband's craft tape."

"The green stripe really brings out your skin tone," I told him.

He glowered at me. "This is a crime scene, not a comedy club."

"Aw, you think I'm funny? That's the nicest thing you've ever said to me."

Grumbling, he turned away and marched across the sand to the surfboard.

"Why are so many people here at nighttime?" I didn't realize what a hot spot Balefire Beach was after dark.

"They're all from the same party at a house nearby," the deputy said. "They said they heard unusual noises and came to the beach to have a look." He cast a glance over his shoulder in the direction of the small group. "It's hard to know what to believe, though, since not one of them is sober."

"And they found the body?" Sheriff Nash asked.

The deputy nodded. "The owner of the house called it in. He's the most sober, which isn't saying much. He keeps tipping an imaginary hat and saying 'top o' the evening' to me."

I stifled a laugh.

"Any chance one of them accidentally waved a surfboard around and didn't notice its owner within striking distance?" Granger asked.

Deputy Bolan scratched his head. "I can't rule it out completely, but my gut says no. They all walked over together and they're too drunk to stick to a made-up story. One of them would spill the beans—right after they spilled their guts."

"Did you ask them to describe the noise?" the sheriff asked. "Maybe they heard a scuffle between Mr. Barnes and an assailant?"

With his tiny hands on birdlike hips, the leprechaun turned to face us. "One said it sounded like a kraken rising from the depths of the ocean. Another one described the sound as a dozen manatees in a barbershop quartet."

The sheriff heaved a sigh. "Right. Maybe you should make sure they get back to the house safely. Make a list of their names and contact details in case we want to interview them later."

"I'll do it, but I doubt they'll remember anything tomorrow." The leprechaun trudged across the sand toward the drunken group.

"Sounds like it was a good party at least," I said.

"On the subject of parties, are we still on for the picnic tomorrow?"

I beamed at him. "Absolutely. Wouldn't miss it."

He crouched next to the body for a closer look. "It'll be all werewolves. You'll be the only witch in attendance."

"As you've said three times already. I can handle it."

He looked up at me. "I know you can, but do you want to?"

"As long as you're with me, I'll go anywhere."

He broke into a grin that ignited flames in my heart. The warmth quickly spread all the way to my fingers and toes. That grin could power a nuclear plant.

"It would be wrong to make out over a dead body, wouldn't it?" I waved a hand. "You don't have to answer. That was a rhetorical question."

Deputy Bolan returned to the crime scene holding a shell in his hand.

"I'm pretty sure now's not the best time for collecting seashells, Deputy," I said.

"One of the drunk guys gave it to me as a souvenir." He tossed it aside. "He says they're normally found farther out in the ocean."

"Then he's not so drunk that he's forgotten his childhood love of marine biology," I commented.

"Someone should be here any minute for the body," the deputy said.

A text arrived from Marley to tell me she was home. "I should get back soon. It's a school night."

"I'm sorry about this," Granger said. "I was hoping the night would go in a different direction."

I looked at the dead surfer. "Not half as sorry as he is."

Chapter Three

I awoke the next morning with a kink in my neck and a dog smooshed under my arm.

It was definitely Monday.

As I picked up the phone to turn off the alarm I'd snoozed twice, the screen lit up with a video chat request from Granger. There was no time to improve my bird's nest and the dried saliva stuck to my cheek. Love is blind, right?

"Good morning," I greeted him.

"Now there's the beauty I fell in love with. Is that a new lipstick?"

"Yes, it's called Plumped By My Pillow."

"Very kissable. You busy?"

"For you? Never."

"I'm heading over to Zed's place to take a look around. Care to keep me company?"

I yawned. "You can't possibly have a preliminary report yet."

"No, but we've got the picnic later this afternoon. I'm thinking I'll get a jumpstart on things just in case."

"Is this werewolf's intuition at work?"

"No, this is a sheriff's intuition at work."

I smiled at the phone screen. "What time will you pick me up?"

"Would you be upset if I told you I'm parked outside the cottage now?"

I laughed. "Did you drive in stealth mode? PP3 didn't even lift his head."

"That's because he's comfortable where he is. Then again, I wouldn't move either if I was that close to your chest."

I jerked the phone higher so he could only see me from the chin up. "I'll make myself presentable. You can wait in the kitchen if you want."

"I don't know. The longer I look at you, the more I'd prefer to meet you upstairs."

"You're on duty, Sheriff Nash."

"Hmm. Raincheck then?"

I blew a kiss at the screen and disconnected. I'd have to come back to the cottage later to shower and change for the picnic. If I had even the faintest whiff of body odor, every werewolf at the picnic would smell me. Talk about pressure.

I threw on a T-shirt and well-worn jeans and hurried downstairs. No time for coffee. I glanced longingly at the coffee pot and spotted a note from Marley strategically placed in front of it.

Forgot to let PP3 out before school. Sorry!

Sweet baby Elvis. I was glad I saw the note. I couldn't leave without taking the dog out first. I whistled and the Yorkie trotted downstairs at his own geriatric pace. It wasn't like Marley to forget dog duty. She was usually so responsible.

I hooked the leash on his collar and ushered him outside. I found Granger lurking by the herb garden.

"Hey, I thought you were coming inside."

"I was planning on it, but I saw this interesting fella." He pointed to the fencepost.

I followed his gaze to the flying squirrel. "Oh, that's Rocky. Isn't he the cutest?"

Granger's brow creased. "Another familiar?"

"No, he showed up yesterday. Seems to like the garden. It's warded so he can't do any damage to it."

Granger cast an appraising look at the garden. "It looks great. You and Marley are doing a good job with it."

"Thanks. I'm pretty proud. I was beginning to think Marley's the only thing I'm capable of keeping alive. Glad to know I'm not a one-hit wonder."

PP3 finished his business and I returned him to the cottage. He ambled toward his dishes on the kitchen floor and I left the house, locking the door behind me.

I saluted him. "I'm officially at your service, Sheriff."

His gaze raked over me. "In that case I really wish I wasn't on duty right now."

I patted his cheek. "Good things come to those who wait."

He grabbed my hand and kissed it. "I'm starting to regret saying yes to this picnic. It only adds more hours between now and then."

I climbed into the passenger seat of the patrol car. "You love hanging out with your pack. I wouldn't want to deprive you."

"I love hanging out with you more."

He motioned to the dashboard. "Music selection is in your capable hands."

I smiled and turned the dial. "Now that's true love."

We listened to *Manic Monday*, quickly followed by Prince's *Raspberry Beret*.

"I can see why you like these old tunes," he remarked. "They're catchy."

I balked. "They're not old."

"Sure they are." He pointed to the radio. "This is the oldies station."

I chewed on that fact in stunned silence as he pulled into a gravel driveway of a mint green bungalow with a shabby chic vibe. The small house was well-maintained and the gleaming white fence suggested a recent coat of paint. Zed appeared to keep himself busy at home between surfing sessions.

"Cute place," I said.

Granger stepped on the front porch and paused to admire the stained wood. "He took pride in his home. I bet you a unicorn's horn that he did all this work himself."

"I'd be a fool to take that bet."

He knocked on the door and waited. "Didn't think so." He produced a key and proceeded to unlock the door.

"Where'd you get that?"

"In the zippered compartment of his swim trunks."

"I guess that's a safer place to store it than a beach full of sand."

He clicked the handle and slowly pushed open the door. The interior was as neat and tidy as the exterior. The farmhouse-style furniture was sparse but in good shape. The decor didn't seem to include any personal effects. No framed photos. No artwork.

"It looks like he only recently moved in," I said.

"Not sure. I'll have Bolan look it up for me." He shot off a quick text to the deputy.

I noticed a new refrigerator in the kitchen. It was an old-fashioned style in the same mint green color as the siding. "I bet this place was a fixer-upper. He probably got it dirt cheap and handled the renovations himself."

"I think you might be right."

Even the walkway had looked new, which was pretty surprising considering Aster's complaints about supply chain issues.

We continued our search of the bungalow. Based on the state of the two bedrooms and limited contents of the master bathroom, it was safe to say Zed lived alone.

"No sign of a spouse or kids," I said.

"There was no marriage certificate on record, so that tracks."

"What about next of kin? Have they been notified?"

"Not yet," he said. "Bolan's on it. Zed's distaste for bureaucracy means there are very few official records on him."

We returned to the kitchen and Granger searched the drawers while I looked through the mail on the round table.

"Nothing noteworthy here," I said.

"I found one business card on the fridge." Granger held it up for inspection. "Gary Markowitz, attorney-at-law."

"The fact that it was fixed to a new fridge suggests he dealt with the lawyer recently, or was planning to."

The werewolf nodded. "I know where this office is. Pretty nice building with a coffee kiosk right at the entrance."

My stomach gurgled at the reminder that I skipped coffee this morning. "As good as Caffeinated Cauldron?"

He shrugged. "Only one way to be sure."

"I'm in."

"Are you sure? I don't want to keep you from your other jobs."

"Valentina's away and Bolan's holding down the fort, right? You need me."

He grinned. "Always, Rose. But it's got nothing to do with my staff."

My gaze lowered. "Oh, I think it has a lot to do with your staff."

He urged me toward the door. "Let's get out of here before I do something wildly inappropriate."

Granger was right about the building. It was pretty nice, even by Starry Hollow standards. Most downtown buildings had a charming historic aesthetic whereas this one was best described as sleek. Lots of glass and angles. It was unusual to find a modern design like this in the paranormal town, but it worked.

I screeched to a halt in front of the kiosk. "Coffee on the way in, right?"

"Would you like it in a cup to go or should they save the environment and shoot it directly into your veins?"

"I love the environment, but I hate needles more," I said.

There was no one in line, so I stepped right up. "One latte with a shot of Wake Me Up Before I Go-Go."

Granger arched an eyebrow.

"I blame 80s music—and Marigold's boots."

"Go-go boots? Do I need to know the details?"

"Last night I had a nightmare that involved Marigold and Austin Powers on a rotating circular bed."

"Who's Austin Powers?" he asked.

"Never mind."

I inhaled the aroma of coffee as we walked to the bank

of elevators. "I think this might be the tallest building in town."

"Except for The Lighthouse," he corrected me. "Hey, did Florian mention a double date this week?"

The doors opened and we entered the elevator. "I'm confused. Florian contacted you about a double date at The Lighthouse?"

"I thought it was interesting. Told him I'd talk to you." He hit the button for the sixth floor. "It's not as though he's trying to sneak something past you. Telling you about the date is sort of necessary to you turning up for it."

I contemplated the information. "I think this might be his way of showing support for the relationship."

"Do we need it?"

"No, but it's still nice to have."

The doors parted and we stepped straight into a law office. A receptionist smiled at us from behind an enormous mahogany desk. He wore a starched shirt adorned with a floral design underneath a blue vest. His wavy, strawberry blond hair was combed to the side and pinned away from his face with a delicate barrette.

"Good morning. Who is your appointment with today?" he asked in a tone that was far too chipper for someone who hadn't finished her coffee.

Granger displayed his sheriff's badge. "We're here to see Gary Markowitz. I'm afraid we don't have an appointment."

The receptionist's smile faltered at the sight of the badge. "One moment, please." He tapped a button on the desk. "Mr. Markowitz, the sheriff is here to see you." He paused. "I'll let him know." The receptionist pointed to a corridor on the left. "All the way down to the corner office."

Granger tipped an imaginary hat. "Appreciate it."

The first thing that struck me about the corner office

was the amazing view of downtown that stretched all the way to Balefire Beach. If I had this office, I'd be too busy staring outside to get any work done.

Behind a paper-laden desk, the lawyer rose to his feet. "Sheriff."

Gary Markowitz was tall and conventionally handsome with an almost comical jawline and a broad chest. Gaston in an expensive suit. His handshake, however, was like being caressed by a flight of butterflies. I wasn't sure if the delicate grip was a show of sexism, but it was better than the savage grip some men used.

"Mr. Markowitz, I'm Sheriff Nash and this is my colleague, Ember Rose. We're here to ask you a few questions about Zed Barnes."

The lawyer's dark eyebrows crept to his non-receding hairline. "Please, have a seat. Everything okay with Zed?"

We settled in an adjacent pair of matching leather chairs. The soft material caressed my body the way the lawyer had caressed my hand. Between the coffee, the view, and the caresses, I was ready to move in.

"I'm afraid we're the bearers of bad news, Mr. Markowitz. Zed died last night."

The lawyer leaned back against his chair. His face registered shock. "Oh, no. That *is* terrible news. What happened?"

"We're working on the answer to that. All we know right now is he suffered an injury to the back of the head. We found your business card in his house. Thought you might be able to offer a few details about him."

Gary unbuttoned his suit jacket. "I didn't know him well. He was a loner as far as I could tell. We only had one meeting and it lasted less than an hour."

"What was the meeting about?" Granger asked.

"He was interested in purchasing a property and had a few legal questions."

Granger frowned. "The bungalow he was living in? Was that a rental?"

"I'm afraid he didn't offer any details during our initial meeting. He was asking hypotheticals."

"Why ask you and not a real estate agent?" I interjected.

"I handle all sorts of legal matters," Gary explained. "Zed seemed to think this particular transaction might end up in litigation. He wanted to know about the costs and time involved. Said he wasn't getting any younger."

"But he didn't say which property he wanted to buy?" Granger asked.

"He said he wanted to take care of a couple things first and then he'd let me know. As a matter of fact, we had a meeting scheduled for next week." He pressed a button on his desk. "Todd, cancel my meeting for next Tuesday at five o'clock."

"What else can you tell us about him?" Granger prompted.

"Not much. Like I said, he kept to himself. The only bright spot in his life seemed to be surfing."

"He spoke about surfing?" I asked.

Gary angled his head toward the view of the beach. "Got excited by the view and started waxing poetic about the surf and sea. I'm pretty sure we conducted most of the meeting by the window."

"They didn't call him the Midnight Surfer for nothing," Granger said.

"Did he have anyone special in his life that you know of?" I asked.

Gary rubbed his chin. "Now that you mention it, he

seemed cozy with the woman that grooms my cat. That's actually where I met him and gave him my card. I was dropping off Jingles and he was there."

"Did Zed have a pet?" I hadn't noticed any bowls on the floor or counter at the bungalow.

"I got the impression he was just there visiting. That's why I wonder whether they had a thing going."

"What's the groomer's name?" Granger asked, pulling out his notepad.

"Tina Foster. Foster's Furbabies."

"Thanks."

I passed him my business card. "If you think of anything else, will you let us know?"

Gary glanced at the card. "You're a P.I.?"

"Yes, and I sometimes work as a consultant for the sheriff."

"She's top-notch if you ever need to hire somebody," Granger added.

Gary tapped the edge of the card on the desk. "The need does arise from time to time. I'll keep it in mind." He looked at the sheriff. "A blow to the head, you said? So you're investigating a murder?"

"Not sure yet. It could've been a surfing accident. Beach was dark and, as he said, Zed wasn't getting any younger."

Gary nodded vaguely. "At least he died doing what he loved best. We should all be so fortunate."

Chapter Four

The pack picnic would be our first official outing as a couple—for the second time—so I was more nervous than usual.

"Mom, you've changed your outfit three times," Marley complained from my bedroom doorway. "I don't think the pack will even notice your clothes."

"Because wolves don't care about fashion?" I asked. "That's speciesist."

Because they'll be too busy staring at your hair and wondering how you got electrocuted, Raoul interjected.

I lifted a spray bottle from the bathroom countertop and attempted to smooth the frizz. I couldn't help my genetics. Not when it came to magic and certainly not when it came to my hair. I'd never be like the other Roses with their sleek white-blond hair and Amazonian height. My looks favored my mother and since that was the only remaining connection I had to her, I wouldn't trade it for all the witchy Stepford perfection in the world.

I adjusted the hem of my 'Broomstick Mama' T-shirt. "What about this? Too casual?"

They're covered in fur and lick their butts. They invented casual, Raoul said.

I peered at my raccoon familiar over my shoulder. "You should talk."

You think I can lick my butt? How flexible do you think I am? Raoul demonstrated his limited range of movement by twisting to the side.

Marley beamed. "Granger bought that shirt for you, so I think it's perfect."

I ran a comb through my hair one last time. "Now I need to grab the potato salad from the fridge and I'm all set."

"Did you make this potato salad or buy it?" Marley asked warily.

I gave her a pointed look. "What do you think?"

Her shoulders sagged with relief. "I've seen what happens when you mess around with mayonnaise and it's not the impression you want to leave on the pack."

Maybe you should offer to bring potato salad to the next Sunday dinner at Thornhold, Raoul said.

I patted his head. "That would've been a good idea two months ago." I set down the comb. "Are you sure you don't want to come with us?"

Of course I do. It's a picnic, isn't it?

I ignored the raccoon. "Marley?" I prompted.

My daughter shrugged. "I'd rather stay here and do homework. You don't mind if Jinx comes over, do you?"

In truth I did mind, but I put on an agreeable face. "Not at all. Your friends are always welcome here, you know that."

Raoul tilted his furry head at me. *What's that weird thing you're doing with your lip?*

It's called smiling.

It's called a stroke. Should I call an ambulance?

I stepped between them and headed downstairs to fetch the potato salad. I felt like a normal girlfriend doing normal girlfriend things for a boyfriend who deserved them.

It was nice.

The doorbell rang bang on time. Typical Granger. Punctual and respectful. Just another reason to love him.

I opened the door and his gaze snagged on my T-shirt. "Looks good on you," he said. "Then again, you could wear a tree trunk with suspenders and it would still look good on you."

"I like the addition of suspenders. My boobs aren't sturdy enough to support a whole tree trunk." I called goodbye to Marley and left the cottage. "Do you want me to drive?"

"No, I don't plan to drink today, not when I'm waiting on the preliminary report for Zed."

I smiled at him as I ducked into the car. "Even when you're not on duty, you're working." Somehow it seemed different from Alec. The vampire's workaholic tendencies were the result of avoiding emotional discomfort and pain. The werewolf's work ethic was more about helping others rather than himself.

"If Zed's death wasn't an accident, then I need to know sooner rather than later."

It was a short drive to the local park where the pack had assembled for their quarterly picnic and to celebrate the full moon. The werewolves had more outdoor events than any species I knew. Any excuse for a tent and a grill. And plentiful kegs, of course.

"There's no band today," Granger said, almost apologetically. "They didn't put in the permit request in time."

I laughed. "You're the sheriff. Couldn't you pull a few strings?"

"If I give these guys an inch, they'll take a hundred miles. Picture Wyatt and then picture twenty more of him."

I nodded. "I see what you mean."

I carried the potato salad to a table laden with platters and containers. There seemed to be enough food for a small army. The temperature was warm enough that I worried about the effect on the mayo.

One of the women manning the table sniffed the air above my offering. "It isn't German," she commented with a hint of disdain.

"No. I didn't realize the ethnicity of potato salad was important."

"That's okay. Everybody knows Lorraine brings German. She always makes her oma's recipe and it can't be beat." She turned toward the woman next to her and started talking about the schnitzel.

My gaze slid to Granger. "So, no potato salad next time?"

"Never mind." He squeezed my hand. "Let's go see who's here."

An assortment of tents was set up throughout the park. A group of wolves played flag football in the open area between them. The smell of a charcoal grill wafted over to me and my stomach rumbled.

"Please say there are hot dogs," I said. I didn't ask for much. A little mustard and a potato roll and life would be pretty perfect.

"Of course there are hot dogs," a voice said. "You're looking at one of 'em."

I pivoted to face Wyatt. "Twice in one week?"

He spread his arms wide. "You can never have too much of a good thing."

"How would you feel if Aunt Hyacinth turned up right now and crashed your picnic?"

Wyatt raised his bottle. "I'd offer her a beer."

"You've got to stop making a nuisance of yourself," Granger told his brother. "It reflects poorly on me and, in case you haven't noticed, I have a reason to win her over." He snaked an arm along my waist.

Wyatt blew a raspberry. "You don't seriously think that'll happen, do you? Hyacinth Rose-Muldoon will no sooner accept you than she'd accept a…"

Granger clamped a hand over his brother's mouth. "Manners, Wyatt."

Wyatt smacked his brother's hand aside. "Than she'd accept a tongue in her mouth. Sheesh, what did you think I was going to say?" His devilish grin answered that question.

"Are Bryn and Hudson here?" I asked, eager to change the subject.

Wyatt gestured across the field with his beer bottle. "They ran into some friends so I left them to it. No Marley?"

"She had a lot of homework."

"Yeah, we would've hosted this on a weekend, but we can't help when the full moon happens."

I looked at Granger. "Are you running with the pack tonight?"

"Depends on work."

Wyatt clapped his brother's shoulder. "You should shift tonight. It's bad for your inner wolf to ignore it for too long."

He sauntered away, leaving us alone.

"If you're not on duty, I think you should go with them tonight," I said.

He pulled me close to his chest. "I don't want to miss out on time with you. I feel like I've missed enough as it is."

"Granger, I don't want you to resist your true nature so we can binge Netflix together. Go. Run with the pack and howl at the moon. I'll see you tomorrow night for our double date."

"Did Florian text you?"

"No, I texted him when I got home from the lawyer's office. He basically said what I thought. He's making an effort because he doesn't want you to think he's biased like his mother."

"I don't recall him making that effort with Wyatt and Linnea."

"You have to remember that Linnea is the oldest. Florian was much younger and way less mature then. I think it's nice that he cares enough to reach out."

Granger nodded. "Yeah. It is. And I like Honey. She seems good for him."

"Honey is a gift from the gods, I swear."

Granger's mother rounded the corner of a nearby tent and broke into a broad smile at the sight of us. "There you are. What are you two doing in the middle of a pack picnic all by yourselves?"

Granger kissed his mother's cheek. "Please tell me you brought your brisket."

"I don't think they'd let me in without it." She turned her smile to me. "Ember, so wonderful to see you here again."

"It's nice to be here again."

Granger winced.

"What's wrong?" I asked.

He rubbed the side of his jaw. "I think I need to see the

dentist. This side of my mouth's been bothering me, but I keep waiting for it to get better on its own."

His mother clucked her tongue. "Typical man. Your brother told me there was a dead body on the beach last night. Is that true?"

Granger exhaled. "Word spread already, did it? I don't know why I'm surprised."

She lowered her voice. "I heard he was found with an axe in the back of his head."

"He most certainly was not," the sheriff replied. "At this point we still don't know whether it was an accident."

"I'm heading over to check on the lemon fizz situation. Apparently a couple of boys thought it would be funny to throw a roll of antacids in one of the bowls." Chuckling, she shook her head. "Sounds like something Wyatt would've done in his younger days."

"Try last week at the bar," Granger shot back.

She shooed us toward a tent. "Go and mingle. Everyone will be glad to see you together looking so happy for once."

"We'll see you later, mama," he said.

We strolled to the entrance of the nearest tent and ducked inside. An older werewolf stood at a portable metal table holding up a pamphlet.

"Your changing body is nothing to be ashamed of," the werewolf said to the assembled group.

I shot a horrified glance at Granger.

"You're pups now, but someday you'll be strong, just like Sheriff Nash." The older werewolf smiled at us. "How's it going, Sheriff? Care to say a few words to the kids?"

Granger offered a friendly wave. "I'm good, thanks. Carry on, Roger."

I elbowed him. "Are you sure you don't want to speak publicly about your experiences with puberty?"

He gripped my elbow and steered me toward the exit. On the way out, I picked up a pamphlet from the table and scanned the contents. "The wolf inside you." The image showed a wolf bursting out of a little boy's chest. I dropped the pamphlet like it was on fire. "That's terrifying. It looks like a scene from *Alien*."

Granger chuckled. "It isn't terrifying to us."

I gave him a pointed look. "Are you sure about that? When you were nine years old and all excited about baseball and Tonka trucks—or whatever nine-year-old Granger was into—you didn't take one look at your future and burst into tears?"

He encircled my waist. "Didn't you see images of childbirth before you had Marley? Did you burst into tears at your future?"

"Yes, and I was terrified."

"Terrified of what?" another voice asked.

I looked up from the pamphlet to see Bryn and Hudson on their way inside the tent. I held out my arm to stop them. "Trust me. You do not want to go in there."

Bryn scrunched her nose. "It's the shifting talk, isn't it?"

Hudson spun on his heel and walked quickly in the opposite direction.

I handed the pamphlet to Bryn. "Leave this on his pillow the next time you need revenge. It'll give him nightmares."

Smiling, she tucked the pamphlet into her back pocket. "Have you eaten yet? The drumsticks are really good. I don't know what Talia used for the breading this time, but it's so much better than her usual fried chicken."

Marley was going to regret her decision to stay home when she heard about the fried chicken. If I was feeling magnanimous when we left, I'd pinch a drumstick for her.

Magic & Midnight

Granger and I made the rounds, stopping for another plate of food whenever somebody insisted we try this dish or that dessert. As I wasn't a werewolf, I didn't have the genetic code that allowed me to eat all day long without consequences. Too bad because I would've liked to sample everything on offer.

"I think I need to leave now if only to stop myself from rolling home," I told Granger, patting my Thanksgiving-style stomach.

His phone pinged. "Give me a minute. Looks like I'm getting the preliminary report on our Midnight Surfer."

I tried to wait patiently for an update. Unfortunately patience was not one of my virtues. I tapped his arm repeatedly until he spoke.

"No water in the lungs," he said, tucking away the phone.

"Okay, he didn't drown. It still could've been an accident, right? He lost control, the ocean spit him out, and the board hit him as he landed on the sand?" I pondered the possibility. "Aren't surfboards light? How hard would you have to hit someone with a surfboard to kill them?"

"If you can kill someone by punching them, I think a surfboard can achieve the same result." He hesitated. "Except they don't think it was the surfboard that killed him."

"Then somebody went to the trouble of putting blood on the surfboard to make it look like an accident."

"Yep, and it was definitely Zed's blood on the surfboard."

If that didn't scream murder, I didn't know what did.

"So if he didn't drown and the blunt force trauma wasn't caused by the surfboard, what's left? A giant clamshell?"

"The report says we're looking for a slightly curved item."

I folded my arms and smiled triumphantly. "See? Clamshell."

He started to smile and it quickly morphed into a grimace. "Ouch."

"Ouch? My joke was that bad?"

He rubbed the side of his jaw. "The side of my mouth hurts."

"You clearly haven't smiled enough lately. You need more practice."

"Trust me, Rose. I've been smiling like crazy since you and I got back together. Maybe that's what did it. The strain."

"It's the first time I've ever been accused of causing excessive smiling."

He opened and closed his mouth, as though testing it. "Might've been the sirloin. It was a little tough even for me. I need to make an appointment with Dr. Kozak when things calm down."

"Don't ignore pain like that. It never goes away on its own and the longer you leave it, the worse it gets."

He offered a half grin. "Are you trying to mother me, Rose?"

I winced. "That's not very sexy, is it?"

His soulful brown eyes fixed on me. "Oh, I don't know. We can put a different spin on it. A skintight nurse's uniform and a close examination of my mouth might do the trick."

"Skintight, huh?"

His gaze skimmed my chest. "Maybe a couple of loose buttons, too."

"So a disheveled woman in white after Labor Day without access to a sewing kit." I gave his sore cheek a feathery kiss. "Sounds right up my alley."

Chapter Five

By the time Granger delivered me to the cottage, the pain in his mouth had intensified. I offered to make him a pain relief potion, but he declined.

"Not that I don't trust your skills, Rose, but I've got a remedy at home I can use that's werewolf-proof." His attempt to pucker up quickly morphed into a wince.

"Call the dentist when you get home," I said. "Please don't wait because the last thing I want is to avoid kissing you."

"Happy to hear it. I'll do you one better and call on the way home."

I blew him a kiss and exited the car.

There was no sign of Marley or PP3 when I entered the cottage. I dragged myself upstairs to change out of my sweaty clothes. Between the warm sunshine and the heat from werewolf bodies, I was starting to stink like an onion in the sun.

I entered my bedroom and jumped back in surprise at the sight of a tall girl with cropped green hair standing at my dresser. "Jinx, what are you doing?"

The young witch turned abruptly, her hand pressed against her chest. "Wow, you scared me."

"Imagine how I feel finding a stranger in my bedroom."

"Sorry, I was just straightening up."

That lie was straight out of Nikki Palantino's playbook. Nikki and I had been friends in high school until she told her mom a broken front tooth was the result of me accidentally hitting her in the face with a soda bottle. The real story was that drunk Nikki's face had an impromptu meeting in the ladies' room with a toilet seat.

"I appreciate your interest, Jinx, but I'm an adult. I don't really need anybody to clean up after me."

She laughed awkwardly. "The state of your room suggests otherwise."

Well, that was rude. Accurate, but rude.

"Where's Marley?"

"She took your dog for a walk."

"It's beautiful outside. Why not tag along?"

Jinx cringed. "And pick up dog poop? No thanks. We have people who do that kind of thing for us."

Right. Jinx was officially known as Fern Green-Wart, daughter of Twila and Jasper, older sister of Shale. She was two years ahead of Marley at the Black Cloak Academy and the two girls had become thick as thieves so quickly, they'd given me whiplash. I didn't love Marley's abandonment of her other friends in favor of the more popular and wealthier Jinx, but I didn't have a reason to distrust the new friend—until now.

Downstairs I heard the front door open and close. "We're back," Marley called.

Jinx shot past me and hurried down the steps. "You took longer than I thought or I would've gone with you."

"That's because PP3 can't commit to a spot. He likes to

test out patches of grass until he finds the perfect environment." Marley glanced at the base of the staircase where I now stood. "Hey, Mom. I didn't know you were home."

"Just got here."

Jinx gave me a guilty look and I could tell she was wondering whether I'd mention her self-guided tour through my bedroom.

"I brought you a souvenir from the picnic," I said. I reached into my purse and produced a drumstick wrapped in foil. "Sorry, Jinx. I wasn't sure whether you'd still be here." And they only let me sneak one drumstick anyway. Granger's mother pretended to look the other way as I hurriedly wrapped the chicken and shoved it to the bottom of my handbag.

Jinx sat on the sofa cushion. "That's okay. I wouldn't eat werewolf food anyway."

"It's fried chicken," I said. "It's not specific to werewolves." I decided to change topics before I got too annoyed. "How goes the homework?"

"We finished," Marley said. "It wasn't too hard."

Jinx blew a strand of hair out of her eyes. "Not for you, genius. It took this mere mortal an extra thirty minutes to figure out the answers to my math homework."

"Would you like me to drive you home, Jinx?" I offered.

"No. My mom texted a few minutes ago to say she's on the way."

That was a relief. I didn't relish the idea of making idle chitchat in the car knowing she'd chosen to violate my privacy.

A car horn blasted outside, prompting Jinx to jump to her feet. "That's her." She slung her backpack over her shoulder. "Thanks for having me."

"No problem," I said. "Tell your mom I said hi."

Jinx fidgeted with the strap of her backpack. "Sure." She left the door open behind her. I suppose she had people at home to handle that for her, too.

I crossed the room and closed the door before PP3 saw an escape route.

"How was the picnic?" Marley asked as she unwrapped the foil from the drumstick. "I can eat this now, right?"

"You might want to put it on a plate, but yes."

I followed her into the kitchen. "Marley, I need to ask you a serious question about Jinx."

Marley stopped chewing and swallowed. "Like what?"

"Have you seen her take things that don't belong to her?"

She frowned. "What do you mean? I once saw her take a pen from a kid in the cafeteria. Not her finest hour but not a huge deal either."

I braced myself against the counter. "When I came home, I found her in my bedroom at my dresser. I think she'd been rooting through the drawers. What did she think she would find in there aside from granny underpants?"

Marley took another bite of the drumstick and continued chewing thoughtfully. "She was going through your stuff?"

"That's what it looked like. When I confronted her, she said she was cleaning up the mess."

Marley snorted. "Well, that's not out of the realm of possibility."

"I didn't care for her tone either."

"She was probably embarrassed to get caught and got defensive."

"Rightfully so. I would be mortified if I found out you were rummaging through someone else's personal belongings."

"Don't make a mountain of a molehill. I'm sure she was just being nosy."

"Then it would be okay with you if she'd gone through all your things first? Maybe read your journal, too?"

Marley gnawed at the drumstick. "Jinx wouldn't do that."

"I just told you she did it to me. Do you think I'm making it up?"

"No, of course not. I think it's a misunderstanding." She tossed the bone in the trashcan. "By the way, have you seen that cute flying squirrel that's been hanging around? Jinx and I saw him outside when we got home."

"I call him Rocky. Where did you see him? By the herb garden?"

"Yeah, but he ran away when Bonkers showed up."

I glanced at the window. "I think he might want something in the garden. That's where I keep seeing him."

"He won't get past the ward. I guess he hasn't figured that out yet."

"He's a flying squirrel. I'm not sure how many cylinders of brain power are firing behind those big eyes."

The window above the sink slid open and Raoul climbed onto the countertop. *You're going to have to invest in a scarecrow for that garden. You've got an invasive species problem.*

The raccoon stood on his hind legs and opened the kitchen cabinet. He proceeded to open a bag of popcorn and help himself.

I watched him with amusement. "An invasive species problem. You don't say."

Before you know it, he'll be eating his way through house and home.

I drummed my fingers on the countertop, pretending to think. "I wonder how I would handle such a situation."

Not very well, Raoul said. Popcorn kernels spilled from his mouth.

"Are you talking about the flying squirrel?" Marley asked.

"I believe so."

Yep. Raoul tossed a handful of popcorn into the air and tipped his head back to catch the kernels in his mouth. *He's a real jerk, too. You should hear the mouth on him. Takes trash talk to a whole new level and that's saying something coming from me.*

I swiveled to face him. "Then we're not talking about the flying squirrel?"

We are, the raccoon replied.

"The squirrel with weird winged arms and huge eyes that look directly into your soul?"

Raoul climbed down to the floor. *That's the one. Freak of nature, that guy.*

"Yes, what a freak for an animal to have anthropomorphic qualities," I said with a wry smile. "Did you ask him what he wants?"

Why would I do that? The guy's a jerk.

"Did you see Bonkers outside?" Marley asked.

Raoul nodded. *That's when the freak show took a hike. Doesn't seem fond of a flying cat. Ran straight across the yard so Bonkers wouldn't see him in the air.*

"I guess I'd do the same if I were him," I said.

Marley headed toward the living room. "I'm going to open the front door for Bonkers."

My butt vibrated and I pulled my phone from my pocket. Granger's photo illuminated my screen. "Feeling better?"

"Worse, actually. I have an emergency appointment tomorrow morning with Dr. Kozak. Do you mind if we interview Tina Foster afterward?"

"Of course not. I can go without you if you're not feeling up to it."

"No, I'll manage. It's a murder investigation. No time for personal problems."

"Granger, you're only human." I paused. "Well, you're only a werewolf. You need to take time for yourself if you're suffering."

"I am taking time. I made an appointment. Foster's Furbabies is only three blocks from the dentist. I can meet you there." He gave me the address.

"Should I bring PP3? He could go undercover for us."

"I don't think we need an insider at the groomer's, but I appreciate the offer."

"Good luck with the appointment. I'll see you in the morning."

"I sure wish you were saying that from across the bed."

I smiled at the phone. "No point while your mouth is sore. Have a good night, Granger."

Chapter Six

It turned out Foster's Furbabies operated out of a Sidhe Shed. I recognized Aster's style the moment I laid eyes on the structure. The curtains in the window were covered in illustrated images of dogs and cats. The material reminded me of Aunt Hyacinth's cat face-covered kaftan. Like mother, like daughter.

Granger affixed his badge to his shirt as he exited the car. "I can't believe I need a root canal."

"I'm sorry. It's pretty high up there on the list of horrible appointments." Although I bet he never had to spend two-and-a-half hours before an MRI fighting his gag reflex to drink an oral contrast.

"The timing couldn't be worse." The sheriff knocked on the door of the shed. "At least it's tomorrow so I can still do the double date thing with you tonight."

"I hope there's a good soup selection."

"It'll taste better if you spoon-feed me," he said with a sly grin.

"I think Honey and Florian might object."

The door opened to reveal a middle-aged woman with

wide-set brown eyes lined with thick lashes. Her chestnut hair was glossy enough to demand its own shampoo commercial. She held a white poodle under her arm, pressed against her hip. It was so small and docile, it could easily have been mistaken for a fluffy purse.

"Are you Tina Foster?" the sheriff asked.

She shifted the poodle to the other hip. "Well, I'm not Gina if that's what you're asking."

I frowned. "No, he specifically asked if you're Tina."

She squared her shoulders. "Yes, I'm Tina. Why? What did Gina do this time? Is it another speeding ticket? Whatever she told you, it isn't true."

Okay, we had to clear this hurdle first or we wouldn't get anywhere. "Who's Gina?" I asked.

"My twin sister. She likes to lay all her problems at my feet. It's real fun, let me tell you."

Tina and Gina. Their parents obviously weren't feeling inventive when they were born.

"We're definitely here to speak to you," the deputy said. "We're sorry to inform you that the Midnight Surfer is dead."

Eyes widening, she met his gaze. "Zed's dead?"

"I'm afraid so."

Tina shifted her focus to me as though I might offer additional news.

"He was found dead on Balefire Beach two nights ago," I told her.

She stared at me in a way that made me feel compelled to check my face for drool or ketchup marks. Finally she let loose a low whine. "Why does everything always happen to me?"

Granger and I exchanged baffled looks.

"I think you'll find it happened to Zed," I pointed out.

Magic & Midnight

"But I'm the one who has to suffer the consequences," she huffed.

"I think you'll find Zed is the one who has to suffer the consequences of being, you know, dead."

Tina tipped her head back and released a growl of displeasure. "This is so typical."

"Um, would you mind answering a few questions?" the sheriff asked.

I felt confident that as long as the questions were about Tina, she'd have no problem answering.

"I guess so." She turned and retreated inside the grooming station.

I entered next. The interior was similar to my office, except Tina had a large sink where my desk was, as well as a metal cage to house her clients. She put the poodle in the cage and locked it.

"I like your office," I said. "Is it a Sidhe Shed?"

Her guard dropped a little. "Yes. How did you know?"

"I have one, too. Mine's on the empty lot over by the sheriff's office."

"I'd been renting space by the pawn shop, but this is much better. My clients love it." Her brow furrowed. "Did you say yours is by the sheriff's office? That's the one Aster showed me as a sample. It looks great."

"Thank you. Aster's my cousin. We almost went into business together, but..."

Granger cleared his throat. "Pardon me, ladies. Any chance we can talk about Zed now?"

Tina pressed her plump lips together. "He didn't drown, did he? I told him to stop surfing in the dark at his age, but would he listen? Nooo. Of course not."

"How long had you been seeing him?" the sheriff asked.

Tina's long lashes blinked so rapidly, I worried they

might get stuck together. "Seeing him? You mean like dating?"

The sheriff whipped out his notepad. "You two weren't romantically involved?"

She scrunched her nose in disgust. "Ew, Zed wasn't my sugar daddy. That's gross."

"Then who was he to you? A neighbor?" I asked.

"No, he was my actual daddy. My father."

Okay, that news landed squarely in my stomach. It had been years since my own father died, but sometimes the loss came crashing down on me unexpectedly, like right now.

"I guess that means he's Gina's father, too," I said in an effort to avoid the emotional detour and stay focused on the conversation.

Tina pivoted to me. "That's normally how human reproduction works. There are three kids. Me, Gina, and our younger sister."

"Nina? Lina? Mina?" I guessed.

Tina flipped her hair off her shoulder. "Gwen."

"If he's your father, why do you call him Zed?" I asked.

"He didn't like the word 'dad.' He felt it came with too much baggage. We didn't even take his name. Foster was my mother's last name."

Talk about issues. "How would you describe your relationship with your...Zed?" I asked.

She shrugged. "We didn't see much of each other. Zed preferred to keep to himself and I'm more of a social butterfly like my mom was."

"Was?" the deputy asked.

"She died about five years ago. That's when Zed started hibernating more."

"In the literal sense?" I looked at Granger. "Was Zed a werebear?"

"No, but my mom was," Tina interjected, "and he picked up a lot of our habits. Four female werebears under one roof are bound to make an impact on you."

"I didn't find any record of a marriage," the sheriff said.

"Because there isn't one. They lived together but never married."

I smiled. "Let me guess. Zed wasn't down with the institution of marriage."

She wagged a finger at me. "Now you're starting to understand him. He disliked anything formal. I'm not even sure he had a driver's license."

"Were you aware of any problems Zed was having?" the sheriff asked.

"If he was in trouble, he wouldn't tell me," Tina said. "We didn't have that kind of relationship."

"Is there anybody he would tell?" I pressed.

"You should really talk to Gwen. She's the one who spent the most time with him. That's what happens when you're the baby of the family."

"Is Gwen anything like Gina?" I asked.

"Oh, no. Gwen's the real Goody Two Shoes of the family. She twisted herself into a pretzel to please Zed, not that it ever worked. She was just wasting her time."

"What makes you say that?" I asked.

"Because Zed wasn't going to be happy no matter what. Unless Gwen was able to turn herself into a surfboard, forget it." She smoothed her hair. "I gave up trying to win him over years ago and I was much better off for it."

I had firsthand experience with someone incapable of being pleased by her family members. Hopefully our new attempt at a relationship would be a better experience.

"What's the deal with Gina?" I asked. "I get the impression she's a troublemaker."

Tina rolled her eyes. "That's putting it mildly. If my sister had a middle name, it would be Trouble."

"Somewhat of a magnet, huh?" the sheriff prodded.

"Not a magnet, the root cause. Gina is the gaping pothole in the road you desperately try to avoid because she will blow your tires and knock out your muffler."

I hesitated to ask my next question. "Is there any chance Gina would've killed Zed?"

She snorted. "My sister is capable of many horrible things—sleeping with my boyfriend, sleeping with Gwen's boyfriend, scamming strangers, stealing from the scout cookie fund—but murder is a bridge too far."

Still, it was worth a conversation with the troublesome twin, too. "Any chance you know where we might find your sisters?"

"For Gina, your best bet is Mystic Tavern. That's where she supposedly works."

"Supposedly?" I asked.

"Anytime I've stopped in, she's drinking at the bar instead of working behind it. She's probably run up a tab she can't pay, too."

"Got it."

"Gina chases a buck like she's part of the Wild Hunt. If there's a more complicated and illegal way to achieve something, that's the path you'll find her on."

Granger jotted a few notes on his pad. "And Gwen?"

"Gwen's the manager of that bakery." She snapped her fingers in an effort to recall the name. "Sweet Dreams."

A local bakery I hadn't yet visited? Yes, please.

"Can you think of any reason someone might have wanted to hurt Zed?" I asked. "Anything at all?"

"Not offhand. Like I said, Zed was a man of few words

and few interactions. He preferred his own company to anybody else's."

"When was the last time you saw him?" I asked.

The poodle barked, prompting a laugh from Tina. "Oh, be quiet, Beetlejuice. Like you would know."

I laughed. "The poodle's name is Beetlejuice?"

"Yeah, apparently she was the puppy from hell, so they changed her name from Taffy to Beetlejuice." Tina pursed her lips. "I think the last time I saw him would've been Gwen's birthday two months ago. She tried to force everybody to get together, but it didn't quite work out. Gina didn't show, not that Zed seemed to mind. Things were tense between them."

"And how was the party otherwise?" the sheriff asked.

"For starters I wouldn't call it a party. There was no liquor and no cake."

I blanched. "No cake?" That was a crime against humanity.

"I know, right? I didn't stay long. Zed's vibe was such a downer. I wasn't in the mood to be depressed."

"And that's the last time you saw your father?" I pressed.

Her gaze met mine and I saw the exact moment reality set in. "Yeah, I guess it was."

I fished a clean tissue out of my handbag and gave it to her. She dabbed at the corners of her eyes, deftly avoiding her mascara.

"We weren't close, but this is still upsetting."

"Of course it is," I said. "He was your father. Just because relationships are complicated doesn't make them less meaningful."

"Are you going to tell my sisters about him or can I do it?" she asked.

"I think it would be better coming from you," Granger said.

She nodded. "I'll call them as soon as I finish with Beetlejuice, although I'm sure Gina won't answer. It's too early in the day for her to be awake."

"If you learn anything new, will you give me a call?" the sheriff asked.

"Yeah." Tina leaned against the sink and sighed. "Wow. I can't believe Zed's dead. What a way to start the day."

"Look on the bright side," I said, "at least yours is starting at all."

Chapter Seven

Later that day I arrived home to find two furry bodies engaged in a front yard brawl. I hurried from the car and ran toward the garden.

"Raoul, stop! What do you think you're doing?"

The raccoon retracted his claws and let the flying squirrel go. *I'm telling you, Rocky is a jerk. He said terrible things about you.*

I laughed. "Are you kidding? Look at that adorable face. Butter wouldn't melt."

Rocky fluttered the lashes that arced over his huge eyes, prompting a groan of frustration from Raoul.

I regarded the raccoon. "Are you sure you're not jealous? You have nothing to worry about, you know. I have no plans to switch up my familiar."

That's not how familiars work anyway. You can't 'switch us up' like you're trying on a new hat. He paused. *Although I would advise you to try a new hat. The one I saw you wearing the other day made you look like you were auditioning for a role in Newsies.*

My hands moved to my hips. "I bet Rocky would never disparage my choice of hat."

Are you kidding? Rocky's too busy disparaging everything else about you to comment on a hat.

I marched toward the house. "Has he said what he wants?"

He wants a punch in the face, which I was trying to accommodate when you showed up.

I spared the raccoon a glance over my shoulder as I unlocked the door. "You should try to be nicer."

Says the witch that sat in her car for an extra two minutes singing to Taylor Swift because someone honked for her parking spot.

"Totally justified." I closed the door behind us.

What's on the agenda today? Raoul asked.

"I don't know what's on your agenda, but I'm having dinner with Granger, Florian, and Honey."

Can Marley and I order a pizza?

"Marley's going home with Jinx after school and staying overnight."

The raccoon looked at me expectantly. *Can I order a pizza?*

"Sure, if you share with Rocky."

Forget it, he mumbled. *I'd rather take my chances at the dump.*

It felt strange to have the cottage to myself in the afternoon. I was accustomed to Marley arriving home and dumping her backpack on the floor, eager to tell me about her day. I knew this was part of growing up and establishing her own identity, but I already missed her.

I went upstairs to choose an outfit for dinner and found myself staring at the dresser. What had Jinx been doing in my room?

Magic & Midnight

I opened the top drawer. There was nothing exciting in there. Then again, she'd been alone in my room for at least a few minutes before I discovered her. She could've been through every drawer and half my closet by then.

I abandoned that line of thought. For better or worse, she was Marley's friend and I had to trust my daughter's judgment. Maybe Marley was right and Jinx was just being nosy. Teenagers often were and I'd lucked out with Marley.

By the time I showered and dressed for dinner, I'd put all thoughts of Jinx to rest. I gazed at myself in the bathroom mirror as I applied a coat of lipstick. I'd learned the hard way that a mirror was required for lipstick application, at least for me. Some women could do their lips in their sleep, but I ended up looking like I'd treated my face like a coloring book.

Raoul was in the living room with Granger when I finally descended the stairs for our date. The two were seated across the coffee table from each other and Raoul seemed to be miming words, the downside of being a familiar that only I could understand.

"What are you doing?" I asked the raccoon.

Raoul's paws dropped down. *Trying to tell a story. Your boyfriend's terrible at charades, by the way.*

Granger whistled at the sight of me. "I have never felt luckier."

I planted a kiss on his lips. "Give it time."

We left the cottage and drove to The Lighthouse, chatting about the investigation.

"I verified Tina's story. Three daughters. A partner who died about five years ago."

"Do you think she'd lie about that?"

"Trust but verify," he replied as he pulled into the parking lot.

Florian and Honey were in the process of emerging from his sports car as we parked. Smart, funny, and successful, Honey Avens-Beech was the whole package. Between his white-blond hair and Adonis looks and her glossy dark hair and toned build, they made a striking couple. The fact that she was a witch from a reputable family was the icing on the cake.

I caught my cousin's eye and waved.

"Who's with Marley tonight? I saw Mrs. Babcock heading out for her bridge club," Florian said as we joined them outside the restaurant.

"She's staying with Jinx. They're going to walk to school together in the morning."

He cast me a sidelong glance. "You don't sound thrilled about it."

"My feelings toward her new friend grow cooler by the day." I told him about the bedroom encounter.

"Do you think she took anything?"

"Not that I could see. It's not like I have anything particularly valuable and her family is loaded anyway."

"Sometimes kids don't steal 'cause they need things. They do it for fun or attention," Granger said.

"I don't see why she didn't take a walk with Marley. It seems strange that she'd rather stay inside."

Granger peered at the shadows. "Speaking of strange..."

I followed his gaze across the parking lot where a woman was hitting a mail carrier over the head with a dead fish. The assailant looked about ninety years old. White curls sprouted from her head and she was dressed in a bubblegum pink tracksuit and white sneakers.

"Well, this should be interesting." I wandered closer to the scene.

The mail carrier had his hands over his head to protect

himself from the weaponized trout. "I'm sorry, Mrs. Jetsam, but you didn't get any mail this week."

"Lies," she barked. As she raised her arm again to strike him with the fish, Granger blocked the blow. He tore the fish from her hand and tossed it in the direction of the water.

"Mind telling me why you're assaulting Hank here with a dead fish?" the sheriff asked.

"I haven't received a single item in the mail all week. Tell me that's not fishy. Pun fully intended."

"It's only Tuesday, ma'am," Granger said. "I think you've got time."

She drew her bony hands to her hips. "But my birthday was on Sunday."

"I was delivering the mail to the restaurant when she accosted me," Hank explained. "I think she's been stalking me my whole route."

"Where did you get the fish?" I asked. Not from the restaurant, I hoped.

"I found it on the coastal path," the old woman said. "It was going to die anyway, so I figured it was better than using my cane."

Granger angled his head. "Go bring their mail while I have a nice chat with Mrs. Jetsam about the consequences of attacking a public servant."

She puffed out her chest. "Do your worst. I'm old. Nobody's gonna throw me in the slammer at my age."

"You'd be surprised, Mrs. Jetsam."

Her eyes glinted in the darkness. "Are you threatening me?"

Gee, I couldn't imagine why nobody celebrated her birthday this year.

She jabbed an arthritic finger at the restaurant. "Hank's

not bringing my mail. He's the one who should go to prison. That's a criminal offense."

"What reason could he possibly have for not delivering your mail this week?" Granger asked.

"Because I didn't tip him at the holidays."

"Hank's not allowed to accept tips. Neither am I," Granger said.

Mrs. Jetsam seemed at a loss for another reason.

"If you don't mind, Mrs. Jetsam, we have reservations inside and I'd really like to keep them," Florian interrupted.

Mrs. Jetsam stared at Florian like he was an angel descending from heaven. "It was my birthday on Sunday," she announced.

Florian pinned her with his megawatt smile and I worried she might pass out from the intensity. "Happy birthday, beautiful. I hope you took time out of your busy schedule to enjoy yourself."

"Oh, I did."

"On the subject of schedules, we don't want to be late for our reservation," Honey said.

Mrs. Jetsam scowled at the witch. "No need to be rude and interrupt our pleasant conversation." She stomped off grumbling to herself, "Jealous hater."

"Do you think she really found the fish lying on the coastal path?" Honey asked as we entered the lobby.

"Seems a strange place to find it," Florian agreed. "She strikes me as the kind of woman that drives around with dead fish in her car, just in case she needs to assault someone."

Honey arched an eyebrow. "Is there a kind of woman who does that?"

Florian offered a sheepish grin. "I may have dated one or two of them."

We rode the elevator to the restaurant at the top floor of the lighthouse.

"Thanks for suggesting this," I said. "It's good to get out of the house and eat a meal that someone else cooked every once in a while."

Florian smirked. "I think pre-prepared meals count as someone else cooking for you, Ember."

"It takes time to heat those things up," I objected. "And I have to push the buttons on the microwave." I pretended to press the elevator button. "You can get arthritis doing this too often."

The doors opened and we spilled into the busy restaurant. The Lighthouse was always a good bet for excellent cuisine and great atmosphere. The view of the ocean was the cherry on top.

We ordered a round of drinks, except for Granger.

"What's with the water?" Florian asked.

"I'm taking a pain potion for my mouth," he replied.

"I thought you sounded like you were talking with a wad of cotton in your mouth. What's going on?"

"Root canal," I answered for him. "Tomorrow."

Florian winced. "Good thing you're getting a good meal in tonight. There's no telling when you might eat solid food again."

Honey elbowed the wizard. "Florian, don't frighten the poor man."

I studied the menu, looking for entrees that Granger might be able to eat without injury. As much as he loved a good cut of steak, he was going to have to forgo that choice tonight.

"I heard about Zed Barnes," Florian said, after we'd placed our orders. "Such a shame. Do you know what happened yet?"

"Working on it," Granger replied. "How did you know Zed?"

"I'd see him at the marina sometimes. He liked my boat."

"The marina? I thought he only came out at night," I said.

"He only surfed at night," Florian corrected me. "He was a fixture at the marina. He'd come by and needle the workers for a half-assed job."

"So he was the hippie surfer version of your mother?"

Florian smiled. "Hey, you two are friends now, remember?"

"Any chance he needled one guy too hard?" Granger asked.

"Put the badge away for the night, Sheriff," Honey advised sweetly. "You're not on duty."

"When it comes to a murder investigation, I'm always on duty," he said.

Florian swilled his ale. "Mostly he talked to the guys about showing respect for the ocean. From what I heard, he caught one of them dumping a bucket of chemicals in the water and gave him a stern lecture."

"No violence?" I asked.

Florian shook his head. "Anyway, this was months ago. Hardly the kind of thing somebody would react to later. In fact, the biggest gripe I've heard lately is from fishermen complaining the fish haven't been biting."

"They might have better luck fishing on the coastal path," I joked.

Granger drank his water. "Isn't that their usual complaint? If they don't catch something, it's somebody else's fault?"

"You don't think it's possible one of the workers got tired of Zed's lectures?" I suggested.

Florian offered Honey a sip of his ale, which she politely declined. "I really don't. Everybody seemed to respect him. The dude was the Midnight Surfer. He was a legend. Honestly, in a twisted way I think those guys felt honored to be criticized by him."

The server arrived with the food and we all took a moment to admire the presentation. The chef here was a wonder. I ogled everybody else's choices before digging into my striped bass with citrus-glazed fennel. The flute of bucks fizz turned out to be a nice accompaniment to the meal.

"Do you have any suspects yet?" Honey asked.

"Not so far," Granger said. "Seems like there are some interesting family dynamics to explore, though."

Florian wore a wry smile. "There always are."

"How did it feel to be back at Thornhold for Sunday dinner?" Honey asked. "Florian said it went well except for a certain interloper who shall not be named."

Granger grunted. "You can say the name Wyatt. I know who he is and that he behaves worse than a colicky baby in church."

"Why do you think he was so intent on coming to dinner?" Florian asked. "Personally I find him entertaining—anything that takes the heat off me—but I don't get why he turned up."

Granger took a moment to swallow his food before answering. "I can't pretend to know my brother's mind, but I suspect it has to do with the rumors going around about Rick and Linnea."

I stuck a fork in my fish. "What rumors?"

"That they're getting engaged soon. Somebody saw

Rick at the jewelry store last week." Granger looked from Florian to me. "You haven't heard that?"

I shook my head. "If Linnea knows, she's being tightlipped about it."

"Do you think she'll say yes?" Honey asked.

"I know she loves him," I said, "but I'm not sure where she stands on marriage these days. It could be that she's not interested in jumping through official hoops again."

Florian devoured his pork medallions. "So do you think Wyatt is sniffing around because he doesn't want Linnea to marry Rick?"

"Wyatt doesn't want Linnea to marry anybody. It doesn't mean he wants to be married to her either, though. My brother's a difficult character."

"No kidding," I said. "You don't think he'll make a nuisance of himself, do you?"

Granger gulped his water. "He's Wyatt. Of course he will."

"We might have to come up with a Wyatt ward," I said. "We can't have him wreaking havoc. Linnea doesn't deserve that."

"Rick's a minotaur," Florian said. "He'll pummel Wyatt into the ground if the werewolf pushes him too far."

"We don't want that either," I said.

"I agree with Ember. Two men fighting over a woman." Honey clucked her tongue. "So archaic."

"I'll bear that in mind if I ever see some guy hitting on you in my presence," Florian told her.

"Please do. I'd be mortified if you started a fight over me. You're above that sort of thing."

"And blood is very difficult to get out of cashmere," Florian said, looking down at his sweater.

Honey looked at me. "Will you and Marley be at the ritual later this week, Ember?"

"Aunt Hyacinth won't let me miss it. We need to put our reconciliation on full display for the coven."

Granger leaned forward with interest. "Can I hear more about the ritual or is it one of those secret ones?"

"I can't divulge the particulars, mainly because I don't know what they are," I said, "but it's a Mother-Child ritual."

"Mother-Daughter," Florian corrected me. "Which means I don't need to be there." He seemed far too cheery about that fact.

"Too bad," Honey said. "Because I will."

I beamed at her. "Great. It'll give us a chance to bond and swap Florian stories."

My cousin's eyes narrowed. "I suddenly regret my gender."

"We all regret your gender at one time or another," I shot back.

"Technically it's a unity ritual," Honey explained to the sheriff. "Historically our coven used it to bring peace, harmony, and healing to our related female members."

"Apparently it's still limited to witches dancing under the moonlight." Florian polished off his drink. "I'll be home watching sports in my boxer briefs."

"That was a visual I didn't need," Granger remarked.

By the time the dessert menu made an appearance, I was too stuffed to eat another bite. I tried to block out the listing of carrot cake with cream cheese frosting. It was one of my favorites and I hated to pass it up, but I also didn't want to be a glutton.

Florian managed to snatch the bill before anyone else could grab it. No wonder the wizard rarely bothered with magic. Between his good looks, excessive charm, and lightning-fast reflexes, he didn't need it.

"That was actually fun," Granger said as we returned to the car.

"You sound surprised."

"I'm not used to hob-knobbing with the Rose family. I wasn't sure what to expect."

"And not an upward pinky in sight. How about that?" I climbed into the passenger seat beside him.

Granger started the motor and glanced at me. "What do you think? Are you ready to hit up the Mystic Tavern?"

"You want to interview Gina now?" I was staring down the barrel of a food coma.

"She works the evening shift," he said. "This is our chance to catch her unawares."

"You have your root canal in the morning. Why don't you drop me at home and I'll take my car?"

His brow creased. "I can manage."

"I'm sure you can, but you need your sleep. I can handle one conversation at a bar. Go home and take a couple painkillers before you pass out from discomfort." I pecked the opposite cheek, not wanting to hurt him.

He parked in front of the cottage and his brown eyes fixed on me. "I can't decide which is more painful. My mouth or the fact that you're not kissing it."

"I'll make it up to you when you're better."

"Promise?" He started to grin, but pain got in the way and he grimaced instead. "Right. I'll catch up with you tomorrow."

"Good luck. I'll be thinking about you."

"I'll be thinking about you, too. Want to know what you'll be wearing?"

I kissed his forehead. "Let's leave that to your imagination."

Chapter Eight

For a random Tuesday night, Mystic Tavern was heaving with paranormals, mostly shifters. I spotted weres of all varieties in the mix. I edged my way through the cowboy hats and boots in an effort to reach the bar.

"What's the big attraction?" I asked the woman closest to me.

She squinted at me like I had three heads. "Tonight's line dancing."

I would rather stake myself in the eye than participate in line dancing. I blamed my negative attitude on my New Jersey upbringing. We weren't joiners and we certainly didn't line dance.

I finally made it to the counter and claimed a stool. No small feat. I squeezed my purse on my lap and studied the faces in the crowd. Given that I'd already met her twin sister, I thought it would be easy to spot Gina.

I would be wrong.

One of the bartenders moved to stand in front of me. "You look lost," he said.

Magic & Midnight

"I'm looking for Gina."

His gaze flicked over me. "Are you sure? You don't look like the type of someone who'd be looking for Gina."

I had no idea how to interpret that. I retrieved a business card from my handbag and tossed it on the counter.

He glanced down and nodded. "That makes more sense." He released a shrill whistle and boomed, "Gina!"

A woman rounded the corner of the bar and I spotted a familiar set of wide-set eyes. They were the same shade of deep brown as her sister's. If it weren't for the eyes, I wouldn't have noticed the resemblance. Her hair was red instead of brown and it was not shampoo commercial material. It was cut in a ragged style that stopped mid-neck and looked like it had been neither washed nor combed in a couple days.

"Why do I need to wait on this one? I'm plenty busy on the other side," she complained—right in front of me, I might add.

"Busy doing shots," the other bartender said. "You can take care of this nice lady." He winked at me and walked away.

"I'll have a burstberry vodka and tonic," I said.

"Figures," she sniffed and turned toward the bottles.

Gina was going to be a delight to interview.

While she prepared my cocktail, I took a moment to study the interior of the tavern. The decor was rustic with wooden beams along the ceiling and wooden panels on the walls. The floor was covered in a layer of sawdust and peanut shells. I expected to hear a lot of crunching sounds once the line dancing started.

Gina placed the glass in front of me, not bothering to use a bev nap or a coaster. "That'll be ten."

I laughed. "I don't think so. The board says cocktails are half price tonight."

She scowled. "Right. Must've slipped my mind. Five then."

Gina seemed to be working every angle night and day. It had to be exhausting.

I paid for my drink with a ten and told her to keep the change. Maybe she'd be more likely to talk now.

"Do you have a minute?" I asked. "I'd like to ask you a few questions."

She motioned to the crowd. "Do I look like I have a minute? It's a zoo in here."

"I'm here to talk about Zed."

Her face hardened. "If you want to sell me a coffin or whatever, save your breath. I don't make those kinds of decisions."

I glanced down at my clothes. Did I look like a coffin salesperson?

"I'm not here to sell you anything. My name's Ember Rose. I'm a private investigator."

She folded her arms and regarded me coolly. "And why is a private investigator interested in Zed?"

"Because when someone is murdered, it's generally a good idea to find out who did it so they can be held accountable."

She flinched. "Murdered? I thought Tina said it was a surfing accident."

"It was made to look like one, but the evidence suggests it wasn't." Interesting that Tina had chosen to soften the blow by calling it an accident. Despite Gina's bad behavior, Tina seemed to want to coddle her. Maybe it was a twin thing.

Gina shifted uncomfortably from foot to foot. "Isn't that

what cops are for?" She seemed anxious to avoid a conversation about her father, which only made me push harder.

"They've asked for my help."

"Is that so? Since when do they outsource murder investigations?"

I met her gaze, unwavering. "How about you let me ask the questions?"

She cocked her head. "Did you say your last name is Rose? Isn't that the same name of those fancy witches in town?"

"We're descendants of the One True Witch, yes."

"Why are you working as a P.I. if you're rich?"

"I'm not rich."

Her gaze raked over me. "Huh. You don't live over in that big mansion?"

"No, I don't, but I'm not here to talk about me."

"Then I'm not sure what we have left to say to each other because I'm sure as hell not telling you anything about me."

I fixed her with a hard stare. "You do realize that's not how interviews work."

Her eyes narrowed in response. "You sound like you're getting an attitude with me."

"I'm from New Jersey. It comes naturally."

She gave me an appraising look. "I thought there was something different about you. What's it like there?"

"Lots of traffic and strip malls. High property taxes."

She snorted. "Sounds like a real dream. No wonder you moved here." Her eyelashes fluttered. "I had a huge crush on Tony Soprano when I was younger. Do you think I'd meet a guy like that if I went there?"

"As long as you stay north of Trenton, your chances are decent. Can we get back to my questions now?"

Her brown eyes gleamed with mischief. "I'll tell you what, sugar. You agree to compete in the line dancing competition and I'll answer any question you ask."

"Why?"

"Because I'd like to see how badly you want this information."

"Is this your version of dance, monkey, dance?"

She smirked. "Like I said, how bad do you want it?"

Her sisters weren't kidding. Gina was a master button pusher.

I slid off the stool to my feet. "Fine. One dance and then you and I can get to know each other better."

Gina wiggled her eyebrows. "Sounds romantic. I'll be waiting right here for you, honey." She blew me a kiss and waved.

I joined the end of the line with trepidation. I wasn't a bad dancer when left to my own devices, but I wasn't great at following orders and that included orders from men in ugly plaid shirts and cowboy hats shouting out instructions.

I'd never heard of a Hoedown Throwdown and I felt mildly attacked by the title. Still, I kept up my end of the bargain. I made a few chicken-like movements and kicked my legs out in front of me. A handsy werewolf tried to grab my butt, but a well-placed elbow blocked his efforts and would make him think twice before trying the unwelcome move again.

Gina was laughing when I returned to the bar. "Don't quit your day job."

"Too late. How do you think I ended up a P.I.?"

She gave me an approving nod. "You're a good sport, honey. I'll answer your little questions."

Thank the gods because my feet were officially sore. "How would you characterize your relationship with Zed?"

Gina idly wiped the counter in front of me. "I wasn't perfect Gwen, but I wasn't a complete deadbeat daughter either."

"Why do you keep describing Gwen as perfect?"

"Oh, you know the type. She's always organizing family get-togethers and kissing up to Zed. Daddy's little girl." Her expression darkened. "But I'm the one who hooked him up with my buddy Lou to get the walkway redone at his new house. Even perfect Gwen couldn't pull that off. She don't have the right connections."

"I saw that. It looks nice."

"Wasn't easy with the supply chain issues, but I was dead set on doing my part to help Zed with the new digs."

Okay, there was clearly a little sibling rivalry happening between Gina and Gwen. Noted.

"His lawyer mentioned…"

She balked. "His lawyer? Since when did Zed have a lawyer?"

"Since recently."

She made a face. "No way. Zed hated lawyers. Called them demon spawn and sons of the devil."

"He seemed to have changed his mind. He was interested in acquiring a property and consulted with a lawyer named Gary Markowitz. Did Zed mention anything to you about a property he wanted to buy?"

She averted her gaze. "No. Zed and I didn't discuss our personal transactions. Didn't discuss much of anything really, except surf conditions. I think it broke his heart that he ended up with three werebears who avoided the ocean. He should've bonked a mermaid instead."

"Is there anyone else he might have confided in? Maybe a friend?"

"Zed didn't really have any friends unless you count the fish in the ocean." Laughter spurted from her.

"When's the last time you saw him?"

Her eyes glazed over. "No idea. I don't track the days."

"Do you remember if it was after Gwen's birthday?"

She scowled. "Who complained about me missing that stupid party? It was Tina, wasn't it?" She made a hissing noise through her teeth. "I saw Zed about two weeks ago."

"At his house?"

"No, mine. He was heading to the beach and came to say hi before my shift."

"That was the reason? To say hi?"

"I know I said we weren't close, but he was still my father. It isn't crazy for him to stop by."

Yet he hadn't stopped by to see Tina, who seemed to have a better relationship with him. Hmm.

"Are we done here? These beers aren't going to pour themselves."

I passed her my card. "If you think of anything else, will you let me know?"

"I won't, but sure." She flicked the card on the counter and sauntered away.

I couldn't wait to leave. I was tired and frustrated by my conversation with Gina. The moment I stepped outside, my phone lit up with a video call from Granger.

"Miss me already?" I noticed his somber expression. "What's wrong? Not another murder, I hope."

"First you need to promise not to go from Starry Hollow to full Jersey in five seconds."

"How can I do that if I don't know what the issue is?"

He blew out a breath. "I don't know how to say this, so I'll just come out with it. Marley was caught shoplifting."

I cleared my throat as though that would somehow clear my head. "Say what now?"

"Bolan is with her now. He called me as a courtesy. She and her friend were caught stealing a hat."

"A hat?" I felt my blood pressure rising. "Are you sure it's Marley? Maybe somebody cast a spell to make themselves look like her? You know, like poly-juice potion in Harry Potter."

"It's Marley. Do you want me to have Bolan drive her home? The owner agreed not to press charges."

"What kind of hat-selling establishment is open this late?"

"I think you're missing the point..."

My head was spinning. "She's supposed to be staying over at Jinx's house. Why would they be allowed out so late on a school night?"

"I have a feeling Jinx's parents were told the opposite."

My pulse quickened at the thought of Marley committing a criminal offense. "Please ask Deputy Bolan to drive her home. I'll be there in ten minutes."

I put the pedal to the metal and floored it to the cottage. Never mind my speeding offense. Theft was worse.

The deputy's car was still parked in the driveway when I arrived home. I spotted the silhouette of the flying squirrel over by the garden, but I didn't have the headspace to pay our new friend attention. Not while I was busy digesting the knowledge that I was raising a future Lex Luthor. Okay, maybe Superman's nemesis was a slight exaggeration. A future Riddler.

I stood outside the door and counted to ten before I entered. I knew I had to remain calm and not lose my temper. Criminal or not, Marley was a sensitive kid and she wouldn't react well to an emotional tirade.

Deputy Bolan sat in the chair across from the sofa where PP3 had one eye trained on the leprechaun. The deputy sprang to his tiny feet when I entered, appearing relieved.

Marley remained still on the sofa with her knees drawn up to her chest and her forehead down. She didn't bother to look up.

"Thank you for bringing her home," I told the deputy.

He patted my arm. "Go easy on her," he whispered. It was a surprisingly soft statement from the gruff leprechaun.

I waited until the door closed to confront my delinquent daughter. I took Bolan's place on the chair facing her.

"I hope this hat was made of pure gold with Chris Hemsworth's picture on it."

No response.

"I'd like to hear your side of the story."

She lifted her head so that I could see her red-rimmed eyes. "There's no side. I did it. I took the hat."

"Why on earth would you steal a hat? And what were you doing in town so late on a school night?"

"We were experimenting with our magic. Jinx wanted to see if I could use a spell to make a target invisible and take it without anyone noticing." Her eyes rounded. "Not that I'm blaming her. I wanted to see if I could do it, too."

"So you weren't trying to steal so much as see if you could do the spell."

She nodded.

"Why not experiment on an object outside that doesn't belong to anyone?"

"Because we wanted a real-world experiment with external pressure. Would I get caught? That sort of thing."

I shook my head in disappointment. "Marley, you know better."

"I wasn't planning to take it home, I swear. I was going to use the spell to put it back on the shelf without anyone noticing."

"What happened? The spell didn't work?"

"I got distracted partway through and the hat turned visible while I had it in my hands. The security owl started hooting and I got caught."

"What distracted you?" I asked.

Her cheeks turned bright pink.

"Marley, what distracted you?"

"Not what. Who. A boy from school came into the shop with his older brother."

"And he stopped to talk to you?"

"No, he just walked by and nodded." She bit her lip. "But he nodded at me. He made eye contact and everything."

I was beginning to get the picture. "And you have a crush on this boy?"

"I don't really know him. He's in a couple of my classes and he seems nice." She lit up as she continued talking about him. "He's so smart. He's always the first one to finish tests."

"Maybe he's the first one to finish because he doesn't bother answering all the questions."

She smiled. "Mom, he's smart. Trust me."

"What's his name?"

"Nolan Basalt-Ash."

"Cute name for what I'm sure is a very cute boy. What happened to the hat?"

"It's at the shop. I apologized and they said they'd let me go with a warning." She dug a tissue from her pocket and blew her nose. "I'm sorry, Mom. I was so embarrassed. I'll never do anything like that again."

"You said Jinx goaded you into casting a spell. Did she try to do the same spell?"

"I didn't say she goaded me. She asked me if I could and I said I'd try, and no. She didn't do the spell."

"Why not?"

"Because she's not as good with spells as I am."

"I thought you told me before she's talented and in all the advanced classes."

"Well, she is, but she's still not as good as I am. She tells me all the time that she wishes she were more like me."

I vacated the chair and joined her on the sofa. "I'm sure she does, sweetheart, but you can't let people persuade you to do things you know are wrong, even if it's under the guise of a compliment."

"I didn't think it was wrong because I didn't intend to steal it."

"What about the fact that you two were out so late on a school night? Did Twila and Jasper know where you were?"

She turned her face away. "We did a spell to make it look like we were in bed if they checked on us."

"And I suppose you performed that spell, too?"

"No. Jinx has done that one before. She's very good at it."

"I bet." I patted her leg. "I think a little time apart from Jinx is in order."

Marley rolled her eyes. "Is this the part where you tell me she's a bad influence and I can't hang out with her anymore?"

"It's the part where I suggest a break from the friendship, maybe spend time with some of your old friends your own age."

"Jinx didn't do anything wrong." She paused. "Fine, sneaking out was wrong, but we weren't going to a party or

Magic & Midnight

anything. And we saw loads of kids from school. You won't believe how many kids have a later curfew than I do."

I gaped at her. "Now is not the ideal time to make a case for a later curfew. And I'm not convinced Jinx didn't know exactly what she was doing, or having you do for her. Maybe she wanted the hat and was using you to get it." An image of Gina flashed in my mind. If I wasn't careful, Marley could get swept along the wrong path in life. I'd never forgive myself if that happened.

"You don't know what you're talking about. Jinx's family has plenty of money." Marley jumped to her feet. "When did you become so judgmental? You used to be the cool mom."

"I was never a cool mom and we both know it."

"Okay, maybe not, but you were always more compassionate and understanding."

"When it comes to you, maybe. Jinx isn't my daughter, but she's influencing my child in ways I'm not happy about. I thought I was doing a decent job raising you, but you're making me doubt my abilities as a parent."

"You should've thought of that before you had a baby so young." She bolted upstairs and slammed her bedroom door.

My heart pounded as I listened to the sound of her muffled cries.

Raoul rounded the corner of the sofa and climbed on the cushion. *That was a delightful conversation to walk in on. What blew up her straw?*

"The trials and tribulations of being a teenager."

I skipped right over that phase. It was easier to keep being the perfect raccoon that I am.

"Do you think I'm being too hard on her?"

You caught her friend rifling through your underwear

drawer, plus she got Marley in trouble with the police. I don't think you're overreacting. If anything, maybe you're underreacting.

I looked at him sideways. "Is that a word?"

Of course.

I leaned my head against the cushion. "Do you really think I'm underreacting? Marley clearly thinks I'm being too harsh."

You want to vanquish your enemies before they become too powerful to defeat.

I sucked in a breath. "Okay, you might be a tad dramatic. Jinx is a kid."

Doesn't mean she isn't dangerous. She's a witch from a talented family, remember. Just like you.

"Not just like me. We're descendants of the One True Witch. Jinx's family doesn't share our lineage." Not everyone could claim possession of Ivy Rose's wand, grimoire, and Book of Shadows either.

My point is that Jinx and Marley aren't typical teenaged girls. They're powerful witches and their trouble might be far worse than teenaged Ember from New Jersey's kind of trouble.

Fair point. My teen trouble was staying out past curfew and sneaking into parties with beer. Marley and Jinx had magic at their disposal. Their potential for damage was much worse.

"I think this is partly my fault. Marley's been watching me rebel against Aunt Hyacinth since the day we arrived in Starry Hollow. I've taught her how to behave."

Raoul shook his head. *Don't blame yourself.*

It was true to a point, though. I'd been pushing against my aunt to establish my independence and Marley was now doing the same to me. The difference, of course, was that I didn't commit any crimes in pursuit of my independence. It would be far too easy to wander off the straight-and-narrow path and ruin her future.

I sank against the cushion as my own words echoed in my head. Ruin her future. That was what my father had said to me when I'd revealed my pregnancy, that I was destroying my future.

"Do you think I should go talk to her?"

Leave it for tonight. Give her a chance to calm down.

I nodded. "Being a parent is hard."

Try being a friend of the parent. That's even harder.

I looked at him sideways. "How is that harder?"

Because it's not about me.

I stretched my arms over my head. "Well, this has been quite an eventful night. I'm going to bed."

Raoul slid to the floor. *And I'm just getting started. I'm going to bring a post back from the dump tonight to start on our scarecrow.*

"Scarecrow for what?"

Don't you ever listen to me? That stalker squirrel with wings. You can sprinkle a little of Ivy's magic on it and make it extra scary.

"Is that really necessary? All he does is sit on the fence and look cute. He's like an adorable totem pole."

Raoul sighed in exasperation. *Don't let the big eyes fool you. That flying rodent is up to no good.*

I peeled myself off the sofa. "I'll have to take your word for it."

I wish you would.

I yawned. "Have fun at the dump. Try not to track dirt in the house and I'll see you tomorrow."

Chapter Nine

I was still exhausted when I awoke the next morning. As I rolled over to snooze the alarm, I felt immensely grateful that Granger's mother had insisted on driving him to his dentist appointment. My good mood was quickly shattered by the sound of the doorbell.

"Sweet baby Jehovah," I muttered, throwing off the covers and racing downstairs. I nearly collided with PP3 who chose this moment to spring to life.

I yanked open the door and squinted into the sunshine. "Really, Marigold? Door-to-door sales? If you bust a vacuum cleaner out of that briefcase, I'm going to have to rescind your invitation."

"I'm neither a saleswoman nor a vampire. I've come for the reason we discussed, to further your magical education."

"Did we agree on a time? Because I find it hard to believe I would've said yes to the butt crack of dawn."

"It's nine o'clock." She swept past me into the cottage. "We'll be conducting our lesson indoors today."

"Why?"

"Because you're wearing pajamas and your hair suggests a raccoon mistook it for a nest."

"Raoul hasn't done that since…Never mind. I can get changed."

"No need. The lesson involves an open flame and given that you're involved, I think it's best to experiment with fire away from the forest."

I grimaced. "Yes, let's burn down my house instead. Much better."

Marigold leaned over to stroke PP3's head. "Where are your other furry friends?"

"Bonkers followed Marley to school and, knowing Raoul, he's sleeping off an intense pizza hangover at the dump."

"Good. Fewer distractions for us." She set her briefcase on the dining table and unlocked it with precise movements. The cheerleader-cum-drill sergeant was back in action.

I peered over her shoulder. "What's in the goody bag?"

"We need to strengthen your psychic muscles."

"I draw the line at attaching a weight to my brain."

Ignoring me, she pulled a few items from the briefcase, including two white pillar candles, a notebook, and a small mortar. Then she withdrew a plastic container filled with herbs.

I glanced at the plain blue notebook. "You couldn't spring for the kind with pictures of kittens on the cover? I guess this is what happens when my aunt is no longer footing the bill."

Marigold set a candle at each end of the table. "Sit. Either end, doesn't matter."

I chose the chair closest to the kitchen and she slid the notebook across the table to me.

"Is this the Little Book of Scribbles?"

Marigold stared at me. "I have no idea what you mean."

"You and Hazel don't compare notes about me? Huh. I always assumed you complained about me to each other over coffee."

"Spoken like a true narcissist."

"Hey! You seem to have me confused with my aunt."

Marigold's shoulders relaxed. "I was kidding. I don't think you're a narcissist, Ember. If I did, I'd be far more concerned about your newfound magic."

I stretched my arms in front of me and wiggled my fingers. "So what's involved in developing my psychic muscles?"

She removed the lid from the herbs and familiar smells assaulted my nostrils. I recognized the scents of sage, cedar, and sandalwood.

Marigold frowned. "Did you just give yourself a literal pat on the back?"

"What? I guessed all three herbs by their smells. You don't think that deserves accolades?"

"Well done, Ember," she said in a monotone voice.

"I don't need *your* accolades. I gave them to myself." I patted myself again.

Marigold exhaled. "As I was saying, you want to practice accessing your higher self."

I gestured to the mortar as she dumped the herbs inside. "If that's your intention, then you've got the wrong plants."

"Oh, joy. The comedian is back on stage."

She lit the candles with a lighter and instructed me to open the notebook. Then she slid a purple pen across the table to me.

"Are you going to ask me to draw? Because stick figures are my jam."

"You're going to use this flame to connect with your higher realm of consciousness."

"Why?"

Her eyebrows knitted together. "Why not?"

"Maybe we don't want to know what's happening up there. Could be scary."

"The only reason it might be scary is because that's where Ivy's magic resides. The more in touch with it you become, the greater your chances of controlling it before it controls you."

I shifted on the seat in an effort to get comfortable. "I'm ready. Ground control to Major Marigold."

"If we do this right, you'll eventually be able to open and close the gate to your higher self as needed."

"So the magic doesn't come spilling out of me at inappropriate times?"

"Exactly."

She lit the herbs on fire.

"Maybe we should open a window," I said.

"I think we'll be fine, Ember."

"Did you at least bring a fire extinguisher in that briefcase of yours?" I gave her a long look. "Hazel would have."

She ignored me. "I need you to focus on the flame in front of you."

"Why are there two flames if I have to focus on this one?"

"Because I'm going to focus on the other one and help you. I need you to clear your mind and lose yourself in the flame."

I tried to clear my thoughts, no easy feat for me when it was such a cluttered place. I strained my eyeballs as I gazed at the flickering flame.

"Ember, you're allowed to blink."

"Oh. Phew." I squeezed my eyes closed. "I thought I was going to need eyedrops in a minute." I recovered my focus and observed the flame.

"Get to know your flame," Marigold intoned.

I nodded at the flame, Joey Tribbiani style. "Hey, how you doin'?"

Marigold seemed to expel all the air from her lungs. "Not like you're asking it out on a date. Note its physical characteristics."

"Like I wouldn't do that for a date?"

Marigold slapped her hands on her cheeks. "The color. The intensity of the flame. How high does it reach? Those sorts of things."

"If I'm thinking about all that, how am I clearing my mind?"

"It helps clear your mind of all the thoughts that weigh you down and ground you to the earth. If you're too bogged down with mental baggage, you can't reach the higher plane."

I rested my hands on the table. "I have a daughter making poor choices, a murder investigation, bills to pay… Did I mention my daughter is making poor choices? It's hard to wipe that from my memories so I can watch a candle burn."

"That's the point, Ember. It's similar to meditation."

"Which we've already established I suck at."

"Once you form a strong enough connection to the flame, you'll attempt to control it."

"I thought we were accessing my higher power, not turning me into the Fire Whisperer."

"It's only the beginning, Ember. A step toward your higher self. All of this takes time and practice." She paused. "And fewer questions."

"You want me to learn, don't you? That involves answering questions."

Marigold sighed. "I guess you're right."

I cupped my hand to my ear. "A little louder for the people in the back."

"Nobody's in the back. It's the two of us at this table. That's it." She cleared her throat. "Let's try again. Once you feel a connection to the flame, I want you to try to move it. Make it larger, smaller, move left or right. Take the shape of a bow. Anything to see if you can visualize an outcome and make it happen."

We sat in silence for a full five minutes with me staring down my flame and Marigold staring down hers. I tried to envision the flame growing wider, but it retained its same form.

"Okay, I think that's enough for now," Marigold announced. She tapped the table with her index finger. "Now I want you to jot notes in your book about your experience. Don't judge your thoughts or try to analyze them. Just write them down."

I wrote *fire hot*. I tapped the pen on the table, thinking. *Wax sticky*.

"Don't think, Ember. Write."

I wrote *bossy witch*. Then *hungry*. "Do you realize I haven't even had breakfast yet? Or coffee? Maybe if I'd been forced to concentrate on a cup of coffee, I might've performed better."

Marigold folded her arms and assessed me. "Have you written anything in your notebook?"

"Yes." I pulled the notebook closer to me. "Do I have to show you my notes?"

"No, they're for your benefit."

Phew.

"This is only the start of your practice, so don't feel discouraged. These skills take time to master."

"Shouldn't I be good at all of them already? I mean because of Ivy, not because of me."

"Not necessarily. You need to build a psychic bridge between the two of you. That won't happen in a day."

A question gnawed at me. "You said before that Ivy resides in my higher consciousness..."

"No, I said her magic resides there."

"What about Ivy herself?"

Marigold looked at me. "What about her?"

"Is she...gone? Sometimes I feel a strong connection to her and I wonder whether she's somehow still tied to the magic."

Marigold leaned against the chair and observed me. "Do you mean her ghost?"

"I don't know what I mean. Her higher level of consciousness is now hanging out with mine while I'm down here in the cheap seats? Is that possible?"

"I'm not sure. I thought Ivy hid her magic in a receptacle. Wouldn't that by definition mean that she separated herself from it?"

I shrugged. "I guess."

"This might be a question for Delphine." She studied me closely. "Are you behaving differently?"

"No, it's not like the Invasion of the Body Snatchers or anything." It was difficult to describe. "I haven't even mentioned it because it hasn't been an issue. I just sort of feel her presence, but not in a creepy way." I wasn't afraid of Ivy. If anything, I felt comforted by the sensation. She was family.

"It's worth investigating, but I wouldn't go around

telling people you're sharing a space with Ivy. It might make them uncomfortable."

My gaze shifted to the flame. "But that would never happen now. Hindsight is 20/20 and all that."

"I'd like to say I agree with you. Unfortunately I've witnessed a lot of darkness that I would've said could never happen in my lifetime." She blew out the candle and began to collect her items. "I'll let you get on with your day. I know you have murders to solve and bills to pay."

"That I do. Will we do this again soon?"

"Yes, but I want you to practice without me. Treat it like you would exercise."

I snorted. "So you want me to never do it unless you're standing over me with a whip or a swimsuit?"

Marigold gave me a pointed look. "If you expect to get a handle on this, you need to do the work. I know you like to paint yourself as lazy, but we both know better." She snapped her briefcase closed. "I'll see you next week."

"You're going already? Don't you want to try another experiment first? Maybe I'll be better at this one."

Briefcase in hand, Marigold strode toward the door. "You don't want to overdo it. Magic takes more out of you than you think."

"Bye, Marigold. Thanks for your help."

Marigold smiled. "How about that? Appreciation. Such a nice feeling." She left the cottage, closing the door behind her with a soft click.

As my gaze fell on the empty chair where she'd been sitting, I realized I missed my classes. I missed my tutors. I'd resisted their help because that was my nature—the result of independence being forced upon me before I was truly ready. But the truth was that I liked their lessons, I liked learning, and I liked them. It seemed that Marley and I had more in common than I realized.

Chapter Ten

Once I was caffeinated and showered, I decided to drive to the one place I considered a judgment-free zone—Haverford House. It was ironic given that the occupants were born during a time when judgment was thrown around like beads at Mardi Gras.

I parked in the semi-circular driveway and approached the brick mansion. Although the large, historic house was intimidating and came with its own resident ghost, I found it far more welcoming than Thornhold.

I only waited about thirty seconds on the front step before the door squeaked open.

"Hey, Jefferson. Is the lady of the house available?" A burst of air pushed me forward into the house. "I'll take that as a yes."

I made my way to the parlor room where Clementine, the ancient cat, was basking in a patch of sunlight on the floor. She squinted to acknowledge me and then went straight back to enjoying the warm glow.

I heard the creak of stairs as Artemis Haverford descended. "Ember, is that you?"

"Sorry for dropping by unexpectedly. It's an emotional emergency."

Artemis appeared in the parlor room wearing a gauzy white blouse and a pair of black trousers. Her feet were covered in black ballet slippers.

I whistled. "Wow. Pants, Artemis? What dragged you into this century?"

She patted her hips. "I was in the mood to try something new. What do you think?"

"I think you look great. What does Jefferson think?" She and her ghostly manservant enjoyed an unorthodox relationship that I preferred not to think very hard about.

"He thinks I look sexy and sophisticated." She blew a kiss to an unseen figure.

"Well, he's right. You could perform a hostile takeover of a corporation in that outfit and look darn good doing it."

The elderly witch motioned to the settee. "Make yourself comfortable, dear. What brings you here? Not trouble with Sheriff Nash, I hope."

"Oh, no. We're good. Great, in fact. I feel like our relationship is much stronger this time around."

She smiled. "That's nice to hear. You two deserve to be happy."

"We're like cheese and crackers. Margarita and salt." I perched on the edge of the settee. "I wish I could say the same about Marley and me."

Her pale eyebrows inched upward. "What's going on with my favorite witches?"

"Growing pains, I guess. She has a friend I don't approve of and it's causing tension. I thought I'd know how to handle these kinds of issues, but turns out I'm clueless." Marley had always been such a well-behaved child. I had no experience with doling out punishment or asserting boundaries.

"And why don't you approve?"

A silver tray floated into the room and landed gently on the coffee table. The porcelain teapot was flanked by two dainty teacups, a matching sugar bowl, and a tiny pitcher of milk.

Artemis clapped her hands, delighted as though the ghost hadn't delivered tea a thousand times before. "Thank you, Jefferson. You're an absolute treasure."

"Thank you, Jefferson," I said.

An invisible hand poured the tea and fixed mine exactly the way I liked it. There was a certain comfort in surrounding yourself with people who knew you well.

"I think Jinx is using Marley. I don't think it's a genuine friendship and Marley's only going to get hurt."

"And you're trying to prevent that?"

I frowned. "Of course. Why would I let my child get hurt if I can prevent it?"

"Pain is a natural part of life, Ember. People hurt us. We hurt other people. Learning how to deal with that pain is a valuable life lesson for her."

"You're saying to let the friendship play out." I blew the steam off my tea and sipped.

"You can't control everything and everyone she comes into contact with. This is part of our development. What you hope is that she learns these lessons early, while you're still there to comfort her." The elderly witch drank her tea. "What do you think this Jinx is using her for? What does a friendship with Marley offer her?"

I shrugged. "I don't know. Clout, maybe, because she's a Rose. I haven't figured it out yet, but she reeks of trouble."

"What did you say her last name is?"

"Green-Wart. Hard to forget that one."

"Ah. That explains it."

My radar pinged. "Explains what?"

"In the hierarchy of witches and wizards, I'd say they're a tier lower than the Roses. It could be they're using their daughter to boost their status."

"So I was right? You think Jinx is a social climber?" If that was the case, she chose the wrong branch of the Rose clan to cling to. We were the black-haired sheep of a white-blond flock.

"From what I know of the parents, they're consumed by social status, especially in magic circles. It wouldn't surprise me if they encouraged Jinx to form a friendship with Marley."

"Then what's with the criminal mischief?"

"It could be that Jinx is rebelling against these orders and taking Marley along for the ride. Or perhaps Jinx is troubled and her parents were hopeful that a friendship with a girl like Marley would straighten her out."

The latter reason made sense. Marley had a reputation for good grades and good behavior. Throw in the Rose element and I could see why she'd be a target for struggling parents.

"Maybe I'll invite Jinx's mom to meet for coffee. See what I can find out. I feel like we need to talk about the incident anyway." It seemed like the responsible parent thing to do.

Artemis nodded her approval. "Excellent idea. That might help you figure out the girl's motive."

"It might also make Marley happy if she thinks I'm making an effort to get to know Jinx's mother." A win-win as far as I was concerned.

"And how's Operation Reconciliation with Hyacinth?"

"Pretty smooth so far. I had Sunday dinner at Thornhold."

"That's wonderful. You must feel much better."

"It's definitely reduced my stress level, although I have another issue that's giving me angst."

A smile tugged at her lips. "Aside from Marley's choice of friends?"

I nodded. "You have experience with ghosts."

She folded her hands primly in her lap. "I would say so."

"Do you think it's possible for a witch to be so tied to her magic that they become inseparable?"

"You mean the boundaries become blurred so that the magic becomes the witch and vice-versa?"

"Maybe. I don't know how to explain it. Say I die and manage to transfer my magic to Marley. Would it be possible for me to somehow live on through my magic and, therefore, live on through Marley?"

"You never struck me as the kind of witch seeking immortality."

"No, I'm not. At all. It's a hypothetical question. I'm helping Marley with a research paper for school."

"I think it's a rare case where the magic merges with the witch so completely."

"But you think it's possible?" I pressed.

"My dear, I've learned in my long life that anything is possible and that just because it hasn't happened to me doesn't mean it can't happen." She sipped her tea, eyeing me over the rim of the cup. "Now tell me, Ember, is this truly a research paper or is this about Ivy?"

"Can't fool you, can I?" As my frequent confidante, I should've known I couldn't get anything past Artemis.

"The real question is—why would you want to?"

"I guess I feel anxious about the whole thing. Marigold is convinced I need emergency lessons to combat the effects of Ivy's magic. Aunt Hyacinth went to great lengths to acquire it and now it's co-habitating with me."

"My dear, it's only natural that you'd want to have a better grasp of the situation, but I'm afraid I don't know the answers you seek."

I waved at the table. "Can't you read tea leaves or Scrabble tiles or something? Offer me a little guidance?"

Artemis tilted her head. "I would if it would make you feel better."

My shoulders sagged. "But it won't help."

She shook her head. "Afraid not."

I stood and stretched. "Thanks for the tea and the pep talk."

"I'm sorry I couldn't be more helpful."

I bent down to offer a peck on her wrinkled cheek. "You're always helpful, Artemis. It's basically your superpower."

The moment I stepped foot inside Sweet Dreams and inhaled the competing aromas of cinnamon, chocolate, and fresh bread, it was like I'd died and ascended to bakery heaven. I drew the line at thanking my lucky stars for bringing me here considering those lucky stars involved the murder of Zed Barnes.

There was one customer in front of me and one woman behind the counter. The woman was the younger, blonder version of her sister, Tina. Those werebear genes ran strong in their family. She spoke to the customer in a way that suggested he was a regular. I listened to his order in case I decided to copy it.

"You don't want the cinnamon croissant today, Donny. You want the cinnamon bun. I've never seen them come out so good."

"You've convinced me," Donny said. "And a large..."

"Black coffee." She smiled coyly. "You don't have to tell me."

I glimpsed the cinnamon bun as she slid it into a bag. It looked amazing. The smell of fresh coffee was even better. Sometimes I loved my job.

I ordered first and waited for Donny to vacate the premises before I launched into the real reason for my visit.

"Anything else?" she asked as she rang up my order.

"Are you Gwen?"

She handed me the brown bag and a cappuccino. "So says my name tag." She looked down at her chest. "If I'd actually remembered to wear it."

"I'm Ember Rose with R&R Investigations. I'm working as a consultant for the sheriff's office."

She made a disgruntled face. "Is this about Gina's pyramid scheme? Because I had nothing to do with it, I swear."

"Uh, no. Nothing to do with that. I'm here about Zed's death."

Her eyelids fluttered. "Oh."

"Did Tina or Gina mention I spoke with them?"

She shook her head. "I don't talk much to my sisters."

I leaned a hip against the counter. "Any particular reason?"

"Do you have any twins in your family?"

"No. I'm an only child."

She grunted. "That's how I feel sometimes. Twins have that special bond, you know? Growing up, it was all about 'the twins.'" She used air quotes. "I felt like an afterthought most of the time." She paused. "I made an effort, though, so at least I know in my heart of hearts that I tried."

"You weren't close with Zed?"

A vague smile passed her lips. "Closer than anybody else was, but that isn't saying much. He'd get close and then pull away again."

"Why do you think he did that?"

"I don't know. My therapist can't tell you either. Believe me, I've tried to pry an answer out of her, but she insists she's only there to listen and not offer explanations." She looked at me and smiled. "I'd pay extra for explanations."

"Tina mentioned that your father...Zed became more solitary after your mother died. Would you agree with that statement?"

"Definitely. He basically only left the house to surf and give the guys at the marina a hard time."

"Did you ever invite him out? Encourage him to leave during the day?"

"Of course. I even tried to set him up on a date once." She blew a raspberry. "That was a spectacularly bad idea. That poor woman is probably still scarred."

Curiosity got the better of me. "What happened?"

"Instead of taking her to dinner, he decided to take her surfing."

"And she wasn't up for it?"

"She couldn't have been up for it if she wanted to. She was in a wheelchair. She'd lost her leg in a tragic broomstick accident." Gwen closed her eyes as though picturing the memory. "Zed was so stubborn. He insisted this poor woman could learn to surf if she really wanted to. Mind over matter, he told her." Gwen buried her face in her hands. "I've never been so mortified. I bought her a dozen roses the next day and a gift card to the Wish Market."

The story gave me secondhand embarrassment. "That's awful. I'm sorry."

"Gina used to accuse me of staying close to him so I could inherit the estate." She shook her head. "The irony."

The house the sheriff and I visited could hardly be described as an estate.

"And did you inherit anything?"

"Don't know. I haven't talked to anybody about it yet. I doubt he had a will. He hated formalities. Anyway, whatever he left me won't be Dusty Acres so it doesn't matter."

"What's Dusty Acres?"

"The farm where we grew up."

"What happened to that place? Did he sell it after your mother died?"

Gwen studied me. "The twins didn't tell you?"

"I'm going to go out on a limb and say no."

"Figures. They persuaded him to sign over the deed to them. To be fair, he was miserable there. Every room reminded him of our mom and not in a happy way, but I was sure he'd move past the grief given enough time and then he'd be grateful for the memories. My greedy sisters never gave him the chance though. They swooped in like vultures."

I frowned. "So wait, the twins live there now? Together?" That seemed unlikely based on my conversations with them.

Gwen's expression hardened. "Not anymore. Gina lost the deed earlier this year."

"Lost it as in misplaced the piece of paper?" Somehow I didn't think that's what she meant.

Gwen barked a laugh. "I wish. No, she used the place as collateral and was forced to give it up."

"Collateral for a bank loan?"

"Not a bank loan," she said carefully.

I ran through the options in my head. "A loan shark?"

Gwen pretended to zip her lip. "I'm not saying another word about it. Makes me too nervous."

"Who lives at Dusty Acres now?"

"No clue. I can't bring myself to go anywhere near the place. I begged Zed not to hand it over to the twins, but he was too blinded by grief to listen." Her eyes closed gently. "I guess it doesn't matter anymore."

I thought about what the lawyer had said—that Zed was interested in acquiring a property that may lead to litigation.

"Did Zed ever mention anything to you about trying to repurchase Dusty Acres from the new owner?"

Her eyes widened. "Buy back the farm?"

"I spoke with a lawyer who'd met with Zed and it sounds like your father had plans to purchase a property."

Tears formed in Gwen's eyes and she clutched her chest. "He didn't tell me that, but I'm so proud of him for even considering it."

"I'm not certain of it, but I have a feeling that's what he intended to do."

And now I wondered whether stopping him was a motive for murder.

Chapter Eleven

As I left Sweet Dreams, I checked the clock on my phone. The root canal should be over by now. I sent a text to Granger to check on him. I slid behind the wheel of the car and was relieved to see my phone light up with his picture.

"How are you?" I asked.

"Missing your beautiful face. When will I see you again?"

His voice sounded funny. "Are you okay?"

"I'm terrific. If it weren't for mouth surgery, I'd be wherever you are."

"Is your mother still there?"

"Nope. Told her I was a big boy and I could take it from here." He grinned. "Look. My mouth is working again. It's a miracle." He demonstrated the opening and closing of his jaw.

I laughed. "Granger, by any chance did Dr. Kozak give you special medicine?"

"I don't think so. Why? Do I sound special?"

I smiled at the phone. "Not at all. Get yourself into bed."

"Why? Are you coming over to join me?"

I'd been planning to stop by Dusty Acres, but it seemed my boyfriend needed a little TLC first and I was only too happy to oblige.

"I'll see you in a few minutes." I tossed the phone in the cupholder and hit the gas.

I let myself in through the front door and found my boyfriend tucked in bed under a crisp white sheet. His eyes were closed and I wondered whether he'd managed to fall asleep in the few minutes it took me to get here.

Sensing my presence, he popped open one eye and looked at me. "There's my girl."

I perched on the edge of the bed. "Looks like your mother took good care of you today."

"She's the best, second to you, of course."

I curled beside him on the bed. "How are you feeling?"

"Sleepy but glad to see you in the flesh." His mouth quirked. "Hey, can I see your flesh?"

"Later. When you're not high as a broomstick. I spoke to Gwen, Zed's younger daughter."

"How'd it go?"

"She mentioned that Zed transferred the deed of their family home to the twins and then Gina managed to lose the farm. I think Dusty Acres might be the property that Zed spoke to the lawyer about."

"Dusty Acres," Granger murmured, his eyes closing. "Sounds like the place for you. You're not much of a cleaner."

First Jinx, now Granger. Whatever. It was true. My cleaning skills were right up there with geometry and cooking from scratch.

"I'm going to drive over there when I leave here and see what I can find out." I brushed my lips against his cheek. "You rest and I'll stop by when I'm done to check on you."

He spoke with his eyes closed. "You're so pretty when you're sleuthing. I hope to see your pretty face soon." His voice took on a dreamy quality.

"Can I get you anything while I'm here?" There were no obvious needs. A full glass of water sat on the bedside table.

"Dr. Kozak is a hero."

"I'm sure he is."

He rolled toward me and opened his eyes. "I forgot to ask how things panned out with Marley."

I groaned. "Where do I start?"

"When did she decide to turn to a life of crime?"

I nuzzled his neck. "I don't know what to do about Jinx. I know I'm supposed to let Marley make her own mistakes, but Jinx is bad news. I just can't convince her."

"Yet. You can't convince her yet. Marley's smart like her mama. She'll realize it on her own." He traced my jawline with his index finger. "Has your skin always felt like worms?"

I recoiled. "I beg your pardon?"

"So smooth."

I bit my lip. "I think you mean silk?"

"Right. Silkworms." He kissed my neck. "Soft, silky worms."

I laughed. "Root Canal Granger has an interesting thought process."

"If Jinx isn't hurting anybody, I say let the friendship run its course."

"That's what Artemis said. You're wise even when you can't think straight."

He propped himself up by his elbow to look at me. "I'm high on life. I've got the best job. The best girlfriend."

"The best dentist."

He pointed at me. "Yes! I'm giving Dr. Kozak a fat raise."

"He doesn't work for you, but it's the thought that counts."

"Hey, now that I'm feeling better, we should do karaoke tonight. I'd be willing to do my Springsteen impression. That's sexy, right?" He booped my nose. "Remember when I did that to woo you?"

"You sang karaoke to woo me? I'm pretty sure that's not the standard mating ritual."

"It was when Alec was in the picture." He scowled. "Alec. I don't miss that vampire hanging around all the time like a lemur."

"A lemur?"

"A lech, that's what I said." His eyelids grew droopy again. "If you'd have married him, I would've ended up like the Midnight Surfer."

The statement pierced my heart. "Dead? Granger, don't say things like that!"

"Who said anything about dead? I meant a hermit. Crawling outside under the cover of darkness to ride the waves and avoid humanity."

"I'm sure that wouldn't have been your fate. You're too strong and resilient, plus you don't surf. Two of the reasons I couldn't let you go."

"You couldn't let me go because I don't surf?"

He leaned forward and kissed me deeply. Unfortunately the romantic gesture was wasted.

"Granger, that's my nose."

With his eyes closed, the werewolf slumped to the side

and his head landed on the pillow. A soft snore escaped him.

My work here was done. I climbed out of bed and adjusted the sheet.

"Sweet dreams," I whispered.

My phone buzzed and Deputy Bolan's name lit up my screen. I tiptoed out of the bedroom and answered it.

"Is he still out of commission?" the leprechaun demanded. "My call went straight to voicemail."

"He's definitely out of commission. What's up?"

"Are you busy? I could use a little help."

"You mean in addition to the murder I'm investigating?"

"I'm in the weeds and Valentina is still out of town."

I hurried to my car. "Tell me what you need."

"I just fielded a call from downtown about a suspicious object they found on the sidewalk."

"Magical?"

"They seem to think so. Would you mind heading over now to check it out? They're right outside Caffeinated Cauldron. I'm stuck at the office with a drunk minotaur that caused excessive property damage in a china shop."

"Okay. I'll let you know what I find out."

I turned up the volume on the radio. If I had to add another task to my workload, I could at least enjoy a few 80's tunes along the way. I cranked up the volume to belt out *Greatest Love of All* along with Whitney Houston. Not walking in anyone's shadow. Failure. Success. Living life the way I choose. Learning to love myself. The lyrics seemed apt for my current situation.

I parked the car at the end of the block and walked toward the middle-aged woman pacing in front of the coffee shop. She wore a pink cardigan over a white blouse and black trousers. Her brown hair was cut in a wavy bob.

"You called the sheriff?" I asked.

She nodded as she fidgeted with her purse strap. "I've been waiting here. I didn't want to risk anybody getting hurt."

"What do you think might hurt them?"

She pointed to a round, shiny object on the pavement.

I crouched down to examine the silver coin. "What's dangerous about it?"

"I don't know. I was hoping you'd tell me. I've never seen anything like it."

The visible side was the familiar bald head of one Dwight D. Eisenhower with the word 'liberty' above it. I reached to flip it over.

The woman cowered. "Don't touch it!"

I stopped to look at her. "Ma'am, you didn't find a magical object. You found a silver dollar."

She cast a wary glance at the coin. "That sounds suspicious."

I picked up the coin and held it in the palm of my hand. "It's from the human world. Nothing magical about it."

The woman backed away. "Keep it then. I don't want it."

I tucked the coin in my pocket. It wasn't worth anything in Starry Hollow, but Marley might enjoy seeing it.

The siren's call of coffee was too powerful to ignore and I made my way into Caffeinated Cauldron. Between a lucky coin and a latte with a shot of Four Leaf Clover, I was bound to have a breakthrough in the case at Dusty Acres.

I was curious to see who now lived at Dusty Acres. What if Zed had stirred up trouble with the new owner? If the deed was now in the hands of a loan shark or someone disreputable, it would be plausible he wouldn't take kindly to trespassers or threats.

"Wait for me. I'll meet you there," Deputy Bolan offered when I gave him the update on the 'magical object' as well as the investigation.

"Don't be silly. You said yourself that you're holding down the fort."

"Sheriff Nash would want me to accompany you."

"Sheriff Nash knows his girlfriend is capable of handling a simple interview without assistance."

The leprechaun heaved a sigh. "Fine, but if the boss gets angry, I'm blaming you."

"He's incapable of anger right now. His emotions range from blissful to chill."

The deputy snorted. "To be a fly on his wall right now."

"He's asleep, so you'd be a pretty bored fly." I turned off the engine. "I'll let you know what I find out."

"Don't get into any trouble."

At the mention of trouble, my thoughts turned to Gina. I couldn't imagine manipulating my father into giving me the family home and then losing that home to someone else. To be fair, it sounded like Tina was also to blame, at least in connection with relieving Zed of his property. I'd never heard of a situation where both twins were evil, but there was always a first time.

Dusty Acres was set back off the main road on about three acres of land. In the distance I recognized the unicorn stables that Marley and I had visited.

The house itself had seen better days. The front door was slightly askew and the chimney was missing a few bricks. I wasn't sure whether things started to crumble after their mom died, after the twins took control of the property, or after this new owner moved in. Whatever the reason, it was a shame. The house had good bones.

I stepped on the porch and bypassed a couple broken floorboards. The damage seemed in stark contrast to Zed's beautifully maintained fixer-upper.

A dog barked inside the house and the door swung open before I had a chance to knock. A muscular man stood in the doorway wearing black basketball shorts and a tank top with a barbell design on the chest.

"Can I help you?" He blocked the barking dog with one of his trunk-like legs.

"Hi, my name is Ember Rose. I'm a private investigator. I was hoping to ask you a few questions about this house. Do you mind if I come in?"

"No, but Buster does." He looked down at the dog. "Put a muzzle on it, Buster." The man stepped outside and closed the door behind him, muffling the sound of the dog's objection. "Mind if we talk out here where it's quieter and you won't get bitten?"

I'd been hoping to see the inside of the house, but I rolled with it.

He gestured to one of the white wicker chairs. "I'm Jack Damiani."

"And you own this house?"

He shook his head. "I rent."

"Who's your landlord?"

"My boss hooked me up. My wife kicked me and the dog out of the house and I was sleeping in my car. When Lou found out, he arranged for me to stay here."

"She kicked out the dog, too?" The husband I could understand, but I drew a line at the dog.

"She thinks Buster barks too much." He paused to smile. "Which is true, but still."

We were agreed on that point. "And what do you do for a living, Jack?"

"I work construction. Lou owns the company where I work. Well, technically his dad owns the company, but Lou handles the crews."

The name Lou sounded familiar. "What's Lou's last name?"

"Giordano. The company's called Giordano Brothers, which is funny because Lou's an only child. When I asked why they didn't call it Father & Son, he cursed at me and told me to mind my own business."

"He sounds charming."

"He's okay. He put me in this house, so I can't complain. I've been doing odd jobs in exchange, trying to spruce the place up. It was down on its heels when I first moved in."

"How long ago was that?"

He followed my gaze to the broken boards on the porch. "I'll get to these eventually."

"Do you know anything about the previous owner of the house?"

He rubbed the back of his neck. "Other than they don't know how to clean, no. Don't know who they were."

"Do you know the names Tina or Gina Foster?"

Jack pursed his lips. "No. Doesn't sound familiar."

"How about Zed Barnes? He was also known as the Midnight Surfer."

Jack's brow furrowed. "Should I know these people?"

"They lived here before you."

"You said 'was' known as. What's he known as now—the Daytime Surfer?"

"He's known as dead."

Jack's face fell. "Oh, sorry. Is that why you're asking questions?"

I nodded. "Zed Barnes was murdered on Balefire Beach on Sunday night. He lived in this house and I have reason to believe he was interested in buying it back."

"Got it," Jack said.

I pulled up a picture of Zed on my phone that I'd found in the latest edition of *Vox Populi*. My old pal Bentley Smith had written the article. I'd felt a pang of loss when I saw his byline. Although I missed the crew at the newspaper, even Alec, I recognized that that chapter of my life was over.

I turned my phone toward Jack. "You haven't seen this man?"

Jack leaned forward to study the picture. "No, I'm sorry. Never met the guy. You might want to talk to Lou. If anybody would know, he would. The guy's got his finger in more local pies than Little Jack Horner."

"Where's the best place to find him?"

"His office is near the warehouses on the outskirts of town, but you're more likely to find him at Glitterati. That's where he conducts a lot of his business."

"What's Glitterati?" I wasn't familiar with the name.

"An adult entertainment venue."

"Like a strip joint?" I asked. I didn't realize such places existed in Starry Hollow.

Jack grinned. "More like a burlesque club. You should check it out for yourself. The fairies are worth the price of admission."

"Thanks for the tip." Too bad Granger was out of commission. We could've had a date night at Glitterati and killed two birds with one stone. It was probably better to go on my own anyway. I was likely to get more information out of a guy like Lou without the sheriff on my arm.

Jack tugged his ear. "So do you think I'm going to have to move?"

"I doubt it. Zed's the one who seemed keen on moving back in and he's gone." I thought about the state of Zed's new house, how he'd made an effort to improve it. I suspected he was making up for what happened here, how he'd let his beloved home fall to pieces. "I know it might seem like this place was neglected, but he loved it and his family made some happy memories here, so maybe put a little positivity into the universe and finish those odd jobs. You might not own the house, but you're its caretaker now." I motioned to the broken front door. "That's an easy one. You could do it today."

Jack cast a glance over his shoulder. "You sound like my wife."

"Maybe your wife had a point."

He sniffed. "Yeah, now that I'm living alone, I've been coming to that conclusion on my own."

"Good luck, Jack." I cupped my hands around my mouth and yelled, "You, too, Buster."

The dog barked in response.

"I hope you catch whoever killed that Midnight Surfer guy," Jack said as I descended the porch steps. "Seems like he wasn't so bad."

I twisted to look at him. "No, he wasn't bad at all."

Chapter Twelve

My hands curved around my oversized mug as I sat at a small table inside the Caffeinated Cauldron. I'd requested a shot of Easy Street to help get me through this meeting with Jinx's mother.

My stomach tightened as I watched the door for any sign of her. Although I was willing to have uncomfortable conversations when necessary, I didn't enjoy them. And now that Aunt Hyacinth and I had put our differences aside, I just wanted a chance to relax a little on the confrontation front.

A witch's work is never done.

The door swung open and Twila Green-Wart entered, her gaze darting right to left. She looked like someone had dropped her in the middle of a snake pit and ordered her to crawl out. She wore a pale pink blouse with the top button open to reveal a black pearl necklace. Her cheekbones looked sharp enough to cut glass and, of course, not a hair out of place.

I waved to get her attention. Her thin lips parted in what must pass for a smile in the Green-Wart household. It

Magic & Midnight

reeked of insincerity. I figured she was feeling awkward about recent events and didn't want to face a tough conversation with me. I understood. I was from New Jersey. I wouldn't want to face a tough conversation with me either.

"Ember, you're so punctual." It sounded like a slap disguised as a compliment. Twila dusted off the seat of the chair across from me and sat.

"Thanks for meeting me. I took the liberty of ordering for you." I gestured to the mug in front of her. It was a risky move given that a witch like Twila probably ordered a lot of things 'on the side' and 'without' and 'nonfat.'

She left the mug untouched. "This place is cozy." Her gaze swept the coffee shop.

"You've never been here before? I thought it was a Starry Hollow staple."

"Oh, we tend to brew our coffee at home. When you import the ground beans straight from the best paranormal coffee estate in the world, it's hard to appreciate anywhere else."

"I promise you've never tasted a latte like the ones they make here. Plus you can always add a shot of something you need like Energy Boost or Focus."

She smiled primly. "Ember, I'm a witch. I don't need some fairy in a green apron to make my coffee magical. I can do that myself."

And I thought Aunt Hyacinth was a snob. This coffee date was going to be harder than I thought.

Twila observed me with reptilian eyes. "Tell me, Ember. What's it like to have all that good fortune fall into your lap? Your story is like a fairy tale."

"Which part? The part where my mother died when I was only a baby and my father spirited me away to another world and hid my heritage? Or the part where my husband died and left me alone to raise our daughter? Or maybe the part where Marley and I were nearly killed in a fire by a vengeful mobster?"

The witch stared at me with her mouth half open. "I'm so sorry. I didn't mean to imply you've had an easy time of it."

"Good, because I haven't."

"For what it's worth, you've done a marvelous job with Marley. I'm sure your husband would be proud."

"I can't take credit for Marley. She was born marvelous."

"I wish I could say the same about our Fern."

Good, the not-so-pleasantries were over. "What's the problem?" Was it the violation of boundaries? The deception? The manipulation of innocent young witches?

Twila tapped the edge of her coffee mug. "Jasper and I feel she isn't living up to her true potential. Same with her younger brother. We keep holding out hope that things will improve." Shaking her head, she sipped her latte. I didn't miss the slight grimace as she set the mug on the table and slid it away.

I chose to focus on the more important matter. "What would you like to see improved?"

"Where to begin? Fern and Shale should be at the very top of their classes. They have a combination of Green-Wart genes. They should ooze magic in their sleep."

"Marley says Jinx is in all the advanced classes and that she's very talented."

"Yes, but we'd like her to be *the most* talented," Twila emphasized. "We've spent their entire childhoods cultivating a strong magical base and preparing them for adulthood. We want more than good for them. We want the best of everything."

"Does that include happiness?"

She scrunched her pert nose. "Well, naturally."

"I mean their happiness, not yours."

"If they're the best, then of course they'll be happy. One flows from the other."

My eyebrows shot up. "Really? Do you think Hyacinth Rose-Muldoon is swimming in an Olympic-sized pool of happiness?"

"If she isn't, then she should be." She sat back and emitted a dreamy sigh. "Sometimes I see the Rose sisters at a coven meeting and I think that's what Fern should be. Elegant, powerful, respected. Instead she dyes her hair green and chooses Honors Portents instead of the Advanced Placement class." She clucked her tongue.

"My cousins are otherworldly. I don't know that you can aspire to something like that." And I happened to know they suffered from the same heartaches and messy lives as the rest of us mere mortals.

"Well, either way, I'm glad Marley and Fern have become such close friends. Fern has always been a social butterfly, but I worried she'd never find that BFF. You know, someone to split a charm bracelet with." She offered a saccharine smile.

"I didn't have a BFF or a bracelet, and I turned out okay." Karl had been my best friend, which made losing him doubly hard.

"Still, you know what I mean. And Fern mentioned that your familiar is a raccoon. How very interesting." Her nose scrunched at the mention of a 'raccoon.'

"It was a surprise to me and it was definitely a surprise to my aunt."

"Yes, her familiar is a gorgeous creature. Yours has a preference for...garbage, I understand."

"Pizza is his true love. The dump is a close second."

Her smile faltered. "The dump."

"Yes. It's not far. You take Coastline Drive to…"

She laughed awkwardly. "Oh, I don't think I need directions but thank you."

It was time to cut to the chase. "Did Jinx tell you what happened at the shop?"

Her fingers danced along the string of pearls fastened around her neck. "Oh, I was wondering if you were going to bring up that unfortunate incident. I didn't want to embarrass you by raising the topic."

"I'm not embarrassed. We all make mistakes. Better at their age than thirty years old. Just out of curiosity, what did Jinx tell you?"

"That poor Marley was desperate for a hat but didn't have enough money with her so she tried to steal it. Fern tried to talk her out of it, of course, but Marley was determined. Apparently there was a boy in the shop that Marley was hoping to impress with her magical skills."

Tension flooded my body. "Funny, that's not the story Marley told me. She says Jinx encouraged her to cast a spell that enabled her to take the hat without anyone noticing."

Twila snorted inelegantly. "My daughter has no need to take anything from anywhere. We give her everything she could ever want."

"I don't think it was about the hat. I think Jinx was pushing Marley's buttons." My grip on the mug tightened. "And I was curious what they were doing out so late on a school night. Marley knows better."

"Fern is given a wide berth when it comes to her schedule. It's how she learns responsibility."

She wasn't even going to admit that Jinx had cast a spell

to make it seem like they were in bed. Twila was in denial about her daughter.

"We had no idea Marley would lead her astray," she continued. "I'm sure it's the age difference. In a couple years, Marley will have the maturity to simply go home at a reasonable hour."

This broomstick mama was ready to chuck the remainder of her latte in Twila's smug face. Marley was born mature. She had to learn responsibility at a young age when I was working crappy jobs and didn't arrive home until hours after school finished. Granted, she spent some of those hours with our downstairs neighbor in the apartment building, but she always did her homework and made good choices—until now.

Leaning forward, I lowered my voice so as not to be overheard by adjacent patrons. "Let me put it this way. Marley is a good girl—an amazing girl—and I don't want her to be influenced by someone with lesser values."

Twila's jaw tensed. "I assure you, Ember, that our family is not 'lesser' in any way. In fact, it seems to me Marley is the one benefitting from their little friendship. Fern is the one with a wide social circle and access to the right parties."

"I'm willing to give this friendship a chance because it means a lot to Marley, but I won't tolerate one more incident like this one. If it happens again, I'm afraid I'll have to insist they don't spend time together anymore."

Her jaw remained clenched. "I couldn't agree more."

I tipped back my mug and finished the rest of my latte. There was always that last bit of foam stuck to the bottom of the cup that I couldn't quite reach without a spoon.

"I appreciate you meeting with me on such short notice, but it seemed important for us to talk," I said.

"And talk we have. Will you be at the coven event this week?"

"Yes. My aunt insists on it."

"Then I suppose we'll see you there. It's a lovely ritual. You'll see."

"You should grab a card on your way out. When they punch it ten times, you get the tenth drink for free."

Twila looked down her nose at me. "That's quite all right. I have no plans to come back."

"The coffee didn't persuade you?"

"Afraid not. If I want to add Beauty to my morning routine, I'll simply reach for a jar of Enchanted Foundation. It does wonders for the skin." She paused, her gaze lingering on my face. "You should try it. I'm sure I can get you a coupon if you're interested. I've spent so much money with them, I think they'd be willing to create a special coupon just for you if I asked them."

I suddenly wished I had a surfboard in my hands that I could wield as a weapon. "I would never have guessed you needed so much help with looking beautiful." I pinned her with an extra friendly smile. "Thanks for meeting me, Twila. I hope next time it's under more pleasant circumstances."

"As do I." She stood abruptly, hefting her expensive handbag over her shoulder, and strode out of the shop.

It felt strange to go straight from the uptight Twila to a place like Glitterati. The rectangular-shaped building suggested it started life as a warehouse, but the glittery facade promised fun and games inside.

A hefty bouncer stopped me at the door. "ID?"

"Really?" I dug into my purse and produced my wallet.

"It's somewhere in here. Might take a minute." I found a library card, frequent customer cards, business cards... "Aha! Here it is." I showed him the cringeworthy photo.

He looked from the ID to my face. "I like your hair better that length." He tapped the card.

"Thanks. I'll be sure to pass that on to my stylist."

He stepped aside and let me pass.

The music was surprisingly loud given that I didn't hear a peep outside. I didn't recognize the song, but it was definitely a blood-pumping rhythm.

The stage featured two fairies dressed in shiny metallic thongs and their bodies dusted in hot pink glitter. There were a few groups in the audience, which surprised me given the time of day. One group of men were dressed in suits. Interesting choice for a business outing.

A server ambled over to me, hips swaying. The fairy wore a bright pink plumed headdress and matching feathers that covered her feminine parts. "You here for the show?"

"Unfortunately not. I'm here to see Lou."

She nodded. "I figured. He generally hires younger, but he might be willing to give you a shot if your moves are good enough. How flexible are you?"

"I can't touch my toes and I wake up twice a week with a cramp in my foot."

The fairy frowned. "You're not here for the audition, are you?"

"Not unless you're hoping to clear the room."

She inclined her head to the left. "Lou's the one at the table by himself."

"Thanks."

I threaded my way through the empty tables to join Lou. He was a beefy guy with facial features that looked squished together. His thinning dark hair barely covered his head. His one hand seemed to have a gold ring on every finger.

"Hey there," I said, seating myself next to him.

He glanced up from the ledger he was writing in. "Do I know you?"

"Ember Rose." I set my card on the open ledger.

Lou scrutinized me. "You're a cop? You don't look like a cop."

"Because I'm not. I'm a private investigator."

He stuck out a chubby hand. "Lou Giordano. Nice to meet you, Miss Private Investigator."

I suddenly remembered why the name Lou had sounded familiar. Gina mentioned that she hooked up her father with a new walkway through someone named Lou. Lou Giordano owned a construction company and had installed Jack in Dusty Acres. It had to be the same guy.

"I thought you were my next audition, but you're wearing too many clothes."

"I'm also not a fairy."

"Oh, we make exceptions for girls who otherwise meet the criteria."

I didn't dare ask what that criteria entailed. A change in music drew my attention back to the performance.

"They're very talented." I nodded at the stage where the two fairies were currently shaking their bottoms at the audience. Their hips moved so quickly that I was sure I could feel the vibrations from here.

"You should see their opening number. The magic is off the charts. I might bump them to the prime-time schedule."

"What kind of magic do they do?"

"Watch. They're coming up to a good bit."

I turned to face the stage as the fairies began to multiply, or at least gave the illusion of multiplying. By the time they finished, there was a line of fairies that stretched across the stage, all replicas of the original two. They linked arms and performed a Rockettes-style kick.

"Fun," I said.

"I take it you're not here for the show."

"Very astute. Do you own this place or just use it as an office because the ambience beats a cubicle?"

"It's one of my businesses."

"And the other is Giordano Brothers, the construction company?"

He squinted at me. "Are you from the IRS?"

I sighed. "No, I already told you. I'm a private investigator."

"What are you investigating? Hang on a minute." He snapped his fingers. "Mariah, we need drinks over here." He pointed a finger at me. "What are you having?"

"Water is fine."

"We'll have two bucks fizz," he told the server who'd greeted me.

"And a water," I called after her.

"You look like a classy lady who might enjoy a nice glass of bubbly."

"What gave it away? The gum on my shoe or the packets of ketchup in my handbag?"

"What brings you to my fine establishment? You need a favor?"

I had a feeling one of Lou's favors came with many strings attached.

"No, I'd like to ask you about the death of Zed Barnes."

Lines streaked his prominent brow. "Who's Zed Barnes?"

"The Midnight Surfer. He was killed on Balefire Beach on Sunday night."

"Killed? Like somebody murdered him?"

"That's what the evidence suggests."

He turned the ring on his index finger in what I guessed was a nervous gesture. "Why would you ask me about a guy I don't know?"

"I understand you bought his house. Dusty Acres."

He grunted. "I didn't buy Dusty Acres from nobody. It was collateral that I was forced to collect on, but not from anybody named Zed Barnes."

"Gina Foster?"

His thin eyebrows arched. "Yeah, Gina. You know her?"

"She was Zed's daughter."

"No kidding."

Mariah arrived with two flutes of bucks fizz and a tall glass of water. She set each one down with a flourish.

"Thanks, doll," Lou said. "Who's up next?"

Mariah glanced over her shoulder at the stage. "Bee-Bee's doing her bubble act."

Lou slapped the table and laughed. "Perfect timing." He raised his flute. "Cheers."

I clinked my flute against his and sipped, hoping Mariah didn't drop any potions into my drink on Lou's behalf. I didn't think so, but the thought did cross my mind as the bubbles tickled my throat.

The music changed to a song I finally recognized —*Rubber Duckie* from Sesame Street. Interesting choice.

Instead of Ernie in a sudsy bathtub with a yellow rubber duck, there was a fairy with bare legs sticking out of the bubbles. The audience whistled and cheered as the bubbles popped one by one, revealing more of the seemingly naked fairy. At the end of the song, the remaining bubbles exploded, filling the room with translucent bubbles. By the time the bubbles cleared, the fairy was standing in the tub wrapped in a towel. She blew the audience a kiss and tiny bubbles drifted from the palm of her hand.

"Cute," I commented.

"That's why she's not prime time," Lou said. "We don't need cute at that hour. We need more sex appeal."

"Would you mind telling me how you ended up owning Dusty Acres?"

"Thought I already did."

"And you didn't have any encounters with Zed, the original owner?"

"I never heard of the guy. Didn't know he was Gina's dad. Didn't know he ever owned Dusty Acres."

"Did anyone approach you recently about purchasing Dusty Acres from you?"

"No, but if they did, the answer would've been no. I got a tenant living there. Wouldn't be right to uproot him without proper notice." He drank his bucks fizz. "We gotta keep these things above board, you know."

"Out of curiosity, how do you know Gina?"

"She worked here once upon a time before she moved over to the tavern."

"What kind of act did a werebear do?"

He hooked a thumb over his shoulder. "She tended bar. Gina was a different kind of performer. Lots of drama, that one."

"Why did she owe you money?"

Lou wiped the condensation from his upper lip with a white linen napkin. "That's between me and her."

I didn't get the sense that he was lying about the house or Gina, and his reaction to Zed's name seemed genuine, too. I felt disappointed by another dead end. I'd been hoping to deliver good news to Granger once he was feeling better.

"I'm surprised you never tried to get Gina to perform with her sister." Identical twins had to be in demand in a place like this.

Lou grunted. "Believe me, I tried. Twins are always popular, but Tony put his foot down."

"Who's Tony?"

"Tony Alvarez, Tina's ex. He cuts my hair over at the barbershop on Cauldron Lane."

"She grooms pets and he grooms people?"

Lou grinned. "Pretty much. Tony's a good guy."

"If he's Tina's ex, why was he objecting to putting Tina on stage?"

"They have one of those weird relationships where it feels like they're together even when they're not. You know what I mean? Like Ross and Rachel when Ross was dating Emily and those other girls."

I smiled. "You're a *Friends* fan, huh?"

"I like to watch reruns when I'm feeling under the weather. Never fails to cheer me up." Lou tapped me on the arm with the base of his flute. "So you're a lawyer. You might be able to answer this one."

"I'm not a lawyer. I'm a P.I."

He inched closer to me. "What's a legal way to off someone?"

"By 'off' you mean…"

"Kill them. But a legal way. I don't wanna go to jail or nothin'. Prison wouldn't agree with me."

My mouth opened but no sound came out.

"I know there's euthanasia, but I think they gotta be sick or something."

I held up a hand. "Let me stop you right there. There's no legal way to murder someone."

He waved his hands. "Whoa, whoa. Nobody said nothin' about murder."

"Mr. Giordano, there's no legal way to off someone. It's against the law. All of it."

He scratched his chin. "Huh. The internet has a lot of explaining to do."

I drained my flute and then took a sip of water for good measure. "I appreciate your time, Mr. Giordano. If you remember anything that might help the investigation, please call me."

He motioned to the stage. "You leave now and you're gonna miss the next act. She's a contortionist."

"I'll leave it to my imagination. Thanks for the drink."

"We're hiring," he called after me. "Tell your friends!"

Chapter Thirteen

I arrived home in time to make dinner before Marley's music lesson.

"Can we skip today's lesson?" Marley complained. "I have so much homework and a math quiz tomorrow."

"It's only half an hour. You can handle it."

She propped her elbow on the table and leaned her cheek against her hand. "I'm so tired."

"You might want to remember that the next time you decide to stay out past your bedtime."

Her eyes lifted to meet mine. "You're not going to lord this one mistake over me forever, are you?"

"No. I'm done." I made a show of dusting off my hands. "What about chicken fajitas for dinner?"

She sat up straight. "Extra guacamole?"

"For witches who finish their homework and do their music lesson, sure."

"Fine. I'll go," she grumbled. "But I'm thinking I might want a break from music next year. My classes will only get harder and I'll need all my free time to study and practice."

"You have the rest of your life to work yourself to the bone," I told her. "You need to fit in the things you enjoy, especially while you're young. It's important to feed the soul."

I disappeared into the kitchen to start dinner. I was proud of myself for making a meal from scratch. Okay, not entirely scratch. I wasn't making the flour tortillas myself. Cooking would never be my strong suit, but that didn't stop me from trying to improve.

I prepared dinner, drove Marley to her music lesson, and had her home in time to finish her schoolwork. By the time she said goodnight, I was ready to crash too. It had been another long day.

I changed into pajamas and headed downstairs to collect PP3. The moment I reached for the dog, his head popped up like a Jack-in-the-Box.

"What is it, buddy?"

The Yorkie dropped from the sofa to the floor and padded to the front door.

Company at this hour? I knew it wasn't Granger. He'd texted me an hour ago to say he was getting an early night so he could get back to work tomorrow.

I opened the door and was surprised to see Simon on the doorstep. He wore an old-fashioned nightcap that made him look like a character straight out of *A Christmas Carol*. I half expected him to be holding a burning candle.

"What brings you here at this hour?"

"It's rather urgent, I'm afraid."

"I figured. You don't normally darken my doorstep at midnight." I craned my neck to look past him. "Is my aunt having a late night Twinkie attack or something?"

"Your aunt is in bed with a sore throat and has requested that you take her place at tonight's Council of

Elders meeting which is happening..." He checked his watch. "In three minutes."

I glanced down at my flannel set of unicorn pajamas. "Do I look ready to attend a meeting of the town elders?" Granted, they convened their meetings in a damp cavern that reeked of oysters, but pajamas still didn't seem appropriate.

"Consider me your fairy godfather, miss."

"If you add 'bippity' to your next statement, I'm shutting the door between us."

He tilted his head. "You should know you've acquired a tiny gargoyle outside your cottage."

I glanced in the direction of the garden where the flying squirrel was standing sentry on the fencepost. "That's Rocky."

"Friend of yours?"

"He wants something, we assume from the garden. I think he's likely the love child of Betty Boop and Rocky the Squirrel from Rocky and Bullwinkle. Raoul insists he's bad news, but I think he might be jealous. He wants to be the cutest rodent at Rose Cottage."

"I think you'll find raccoons are an entirely separate order from rodents."

I waved a dismissive hand. "Whatever. They're all furballs that would eat my trash if I let them."

Simon tapped his watch. "The clock is ticking, Miss Ember."

"I can't believe she's chosen me to represent her. We really must be on the mend."

"Master Florian is entertaining Miss Avens-Beech in his man cave, Miss Linnea is with her paramour, and Miss Aster is currently sandwiched between her two sons in a California king."

"Last choice. Got it. You know, she could just miss out on the meeting and not have a Rose representative."

Simon fixed me with a blank stare.

"Yeah, I can see how that might not be a persuasive argument with her." As I turned toward the stairs to get changed, a thought occurred to me. "You know what? Let me try something while I have the chance."

I closed my eyes and tried to harness the swirling ball of magic inside me. Once I felt the connection click into place, I concentrated on my pajamas.

"How very Hyacinth of you," Simon remarked.

I looked down at my clothing, which had morphed into a kaftan complete with the same unicorn images as the pajamas. He was right. It was a page straight out of Aunt Hyacinth's fashion catalogue.

"Maybe I should throw on a wig and pretend to be her." I remembered our recent experience where we swapped bodies during a dangerous moment. "On second thought, been there, expelled the poison."

He moved aside so that I had a clear view of the pegasus on the front lawn. "Your carriage awaits."

"Firefly!"

"It's your best bet to get there quickly and without injury."

The location of the meetings meant that broomsticks were out of the question. No place for a decent landing. Firefly had the benefit of four hooves in addition to a pair of wings.

I gestured to my kaftan. "I guess I'm riding sidesaddle."

"I'm happy to await your return in case Miss Marley awakens during your absence." He held up a bag. "I packed a midnight snack and a book."

"Which book?" I was always interested to know what others were reading.

He tapped his watch again.

"Right. Going." I hurried toward the pegasus and climbed on the creature's back. I'd like to say it was easy and I was graceful, but that would be a lie. By the time we reached the woods, I was hanging off the side and praying a strong gust of wind didn't knock me on my bottom.

I was relieved when we arrived at the cave without incident. My feet landed on solid ground and I was glad I had the foresight to put on a pair of actual shoes on my way out.

I ran to the cave and only managed to trip once without falling over. Score.

Victorine Del Bianco was the first to notice me. "Ember, what a nice surprise," the vampire said.

I stopped panting long enough to greet everyone. "Sorry for the late entrance. I'm sitting in for Aunt Hyacinth tonight. She isn't feeling well."

"It's my lucky night." Mervin O'Malley patted the empty seat beside him. "There's room right here, sweetness."

I hurried to the empty seat and listened as Arthur Rutledge read the minutes from the last meeting. The older werewolf offered me a nod of acknowledgment as he finished.

Victorine's gaze swept the cave. "What about new business?"

Mervin raised a finger. "I don't know if this counts as new business, but I'm curious to know whether Ember here will go back to the newspaper now that she's back in Hyacinth's good graces."

"More like she's back in mine," I said, "but no. I don't think a return to the paper is in my future." I didn't want to discuss my reasons. My relationship with Alec was nobody's business.

"A shame. I thought you did a wonderful job there," Mervin said.

"Thank you. That's kind of you to say. Right now I'm enjoying my freedom as my own boss." Okay, arguably my own boss. Raoul would probably beg to differ.

"I hear you're working on the murder investigation as a consultant," Victorine said. "Must be nice to work alongside your beau."

"We make a great team."

"I wish there was a great team in place to handle the recent issues in town," Oliver Dagwood complained.

Victorine winked at the wizard. "A clever segue to actual new business."

"What issues?" I asked.

Oliver waved a hand in frustration. "Where to begin? The supply chain is a nightmare, there's been an increase in criminal activity, and our beautiful beach is eroding. Anybody who doesn't believe in climate change needs to pay a visit to Balefire Beach."

I blinked. "I was just there the other night. I didn't notice anything unusual." To be fair, it was pitch black and I nearly fell on my face, so I probably wouldn't have noticed. "I didn't notice erosion, but I did see evidence of tire tracks."

"And vehicles on the beach aren't helping matters," Oliver moaned.

"What are the signs of erosion? I was pregnant for that science lesson."

"The sheriff can't do anything about erosion," Amaryllis Elderflower interrupted. "Or the supply chain issues for that matter. Even those of us with magic can't fix those problems."

"I didn't say we need the sheriff," Oliver countered. "I said we need a great team in place to tackle these problems."

"Amaryllis is right," Misty Brookline chimed in. "These problems extend far beyond our sweet little town of Starry Hollow. I was visiting family in Shimmer Falls last month and they were complaining about the supply chain issues as well." The fairy representative tightened the cloak around her shoulders. "We just have to ride it out."

Amaryllis nodded. "As my grandmother used to say, this too shall pass."

"Maybe the supply chain issue will pass, but the crime and the erosion won't simply go away without intervention," Oliver said. The wizard seemed unusually agitated tonight.

"Do we have the most recent crime stats?" Victorine asked. She turned to me. "Is that something you would know, Ember?"

"Not offhand," I replied. I certainly hoped nobody knew about Marley's brush with theft. In his current mood, Oliver would want a great team in place to handle her, too.

"I thought hiring a second deputy would improve matters, but they only seem worse," Oliver complained.

"Maybe it's time for new leadership," Amaryllis suggested.

Arthur recoiled. "Let's not be hasty. I think we can all agree the sheriff does a marvelous job."

Oliver pinned him with a steely gaze. "Can we? I know you werewolves tend to stick together, but surely you don't think this crime wave is unavoidable."

I felt myself getting defensive on Granger's behalf. "You keep talking about this crime wave, but I haven't seen evidence of it."

Oliver harrumphed. "That's because you haven't been a victim."

Now we were getting to the heart of the matter.

Misty gazed at the wizard with the right amount of sympathy. Another twitch of a facial feature and she'd veer into pity. "What happened, Oliver?"

The wizard's eyes turned downcast. "As you know from previous meetings, I've taken up sculpting." Oliver met my curious gaze. "The healer recommended I find a hobby to reduce stress. I find sculpting very relaxing."

Amaryllis pivoted toward me. "You should see his work. He's a natural. I bought one of his sculptures for my garden."

"Did someone steal a sculpture?" I asked.

"Not only did they steal completed sculptures, they also stole all my materials, including a half-finished piece." He pressed a fist to his chest. "It's like they ripped out a piece of my soul."

I exchanged glances with Mervin. I never would've pegged the older wizard for an artist.

"Did you report the theft to the sheriff?" Misty asked.

"I spoke to Bolan, but they're so busy right now, especially with the murder." Oliver looked at me. "Any chance they're close to arresting the killer?"

I didn't dare tell them about Granger's root canal and Deputy Pitt's absence. Oliver might break down in tears and demand their resignation.

"We've been interviewing suspects and have a few leads." It wasn't exactly a lie. We had them; they just didn't pan out.

"See?" Misty said, looking at Oliver with an encouraging expression. "That's good news."

"I'll personally tell the sheriff about your missing sculptures," I said.

Relief shone in Oliver's eyes. "Please, and be sure to mention they're made from limestone. The material isn't cheap, especially right now, and my homeowner's insurance won't cover the loss because I kept the materials outside." He shook his head sadly. "Lesson learned."

"You should talk to my cousin Aster about a Sidhe Shed for your sculptures and materials. You could even work out there if you built one large enough." Of course, Aster was also a victim of the supply chain shortage right now. Hopefully the issues would be resolved soon.

Oliver licked his lips. "Yes, Hyacinth has mentioned Aster's new business venture. It seems like an excellent idea."

"I have one and it's great," I said. "And I met with someone the other day using one for her grooming business. The sheds are very customizable."

Oliver seemed to take the suggestion on board. "I can ward the shed, too, to prevent another theft."

Misty patted his arm. "This is why it's good to talk about what's upsetting you. The hive mind was able to offer a solution."

"I hope I get my sculptures back," Oliver said. "I can't imagine why anybody would want one that was only partially finished."

"Perhaps they could see your genius at work," Victorine said. The vampire clapped her bejeweled hands, clearly finished with our effort to placate the wizard. "It's getting late. Let's move on to the next topic."

Mervin leaned over and whispered, "I'm glad to see you here tonight, Ember. I was beginning to worry the two of you would never work things out."

"I wasn't sure either," I admitted.

"The fact that she sent you as her replacement speaks volumes."

I gave him a wry smile. "It speaks to the fact that all three of her children have busier lives than I do, at least at midnight."

Mervin patted my hand. "Don't fool yourself. Hyacinth Rose-Muldoon doesn't do anything she doesn't want to. If she sent you to take her seat, it's because she wanted to and not because she had no other choice."

I smiled. "I guess you're right."

"Of course I'm right," he whispered. "I'm a leprechaun. We're always right. Just ask Deputy Bolan."

"I'll take your word for it."

I took copious notes throughout the remainder of the meeting so that I had something to present to Aunt Hyacinth tomorrow. Knowing that she'd put her trust in me, I didn't want to disappoint her. As tough and independent as I was, there would always be a part of me that longed to please her. For better or worse, Hyacinth was the only parental figure I had left and now that we'd reconciled, I was determined to make the most of it.

Chapter Fourteen

Morning came far too soon. The sound of my phone startled me awake. As I groped for the phone, I whacked my hand on the corner of the bedside table in the process. PP3 barked, whether in sympathy for my injury or annoyance about the noise, I wasn't sure.

Deputy Bolan's name darkened my screen. It was far too early to communicate in general, let alone with the frosty leprechaun.

I hit the speaker button. "Good morning, sunshine. What now? Somebody found a paperclip and they're worried it'll magically keep their papers together?"

"Funny. You should take that act on the road."

"I was thinking you and I could perform together. I'd sit you on my knee and pretend I'm a ventriloquist."

"And that makes me the dummy? I'm going to pretend I didn't hear you suggest that."

I pushed myself to a seated position and leaned against the headboard. "What's the emergency?"

"We got a call from Morty Henderson over at 82

Starlight. Would you mind swinging by? It doesn't sound serious, so I don't want to bother the sheriff and I'm knee-deep in work."

I bit my lip.

"You're refraining from a leprechaun joke right now, aren't you?"

It took all my strength not to burst into laughter. "No, no. Not at all. Did Mr. Henderson say what the issue is?"

"Somebody broke into his house and stole something. That's all I got."

Another thief in the night. "Okay, I'll take care of it. While we're on the subject of burglary, did you manage to investigate Oliver Dagwood's missing sculptures? He said he reported the theft to you."

The deputy heaved a sigh into the phone. "Not yet. It's on my list."

"Listen, I have no doubt Granger will be back on duty today. When's Pitt back in town?"

"Sunday."

"It'll be here before you know it."

"I hope so. I like having somebody to give the grunt work to."

I clicked off the phone and tossed it next to me on the bed. I didn't know how Aunt Hyacinth managed to attend council meetings in the middle of the night and still function like a normal witch the next day. My body felt like I'd taken it out dancing 'til dawn and fed it a pitcher of margaritas.

If only.

Marley had already gone to school and I was pleased to note she'd taken PP3 outside before she left. That was the responsible Marley I knew.

I chugged a vat of coffee in between bites of elderberry

waffle. If Mr. Henderson wanted me at my best, he had to wait for the caffeine to kick in.

As I left the cottage, I noticed the flying squirrel was nowhere to be seen. Maybe he'd finally given up his quest for—whatever it was he wanted. Too bad. The cute little critter was growing on me.

I arrived at Mr. Henderson's house with the windows down and music blasting, not the most professional entrance. I quickly turned down the volume.

The farmhouse-style home reminded me of Dusty Acres, although this place was in better shape. For starters, the door was intact.

I used my official-sounding knock on the screen door, which consisted of three successive raps. A grey-haired man in a white T-shirt and overalls opened the interior door and peered at me.

"Mr. Henderson? I'm Ember Rose. I understand you reported a midnight visitor."

He looked me up and down. "What kind of sheriff are you? You're not even wearing a uniform."

"I'm not a sheriff. I'm a private investigator. Sometimes I work as a consultant for local law enforcement and this happens to be one of those times."

"That's too bad. I was hoping they might send the good-looking one with the nice figure."

"I'm afraid Deputy Bolan is otherwise engaged at the moment."

"Bolan? I thought that was the leprechaun."

I played innocent. "Oh, isn't that who you meant?"

He glowered. "I guess you'll do. Come on in."

The screen door opened straight into the kitchen. The yellow linoleum floor had faded to a near white and the oak table was covered in a busy floral tablecloth. The room smelled of dried flower petals and a hint of cinnamon. I was glad I'd eaten because the smell of cinnamon immediately evoked thoughts of Sweet Dreams bakery.

"How can I help you, Mr. Henderson?" I asked, trying my best not to salivate over imaginary cinnamon rolls.

His sniff was loud enough to raise the dead. "Some good-for-nothin' thief stole an entire box of cider donuts straight off the kitchen counter last night." He plucked his suspenders. "I knew this town was going to the underworld on a bobsled, and this brazen act proves it. Sheriff Nash needs to get things under control if he expects to keep that badge of his."

My mind was still stuck on the cider donuts. "What else is missing?"

His arm flailed. "What else needs to be missing? I'm not talking about a single donut. It was a whole box of donuts. They make 'em homemade over at Unicorn Farms and they only offer them once a week."

The sound of footsteps interrupted us and a woman appeared in the doorway adjacent to the living room. Her honey-colored hair was pulled into a messy bun and I felt a pang of envy at the sight of her flannel pajamas. What I wouldn't give to be back in my pajamas under the covers right now. I quickly reminded myself I was doing this as a favor for Granger and that quelled the green-eyed monster.

The woman's eyes sharpened. "Who's this?"

"Ember Rose. R&R Investigations," Mr. Henderson said.

She gave him an incredulous look. "Why've you got a P.I. here, Morty?"

"We had a break-in last night." He looked at me. "This is my wife, June. She wouldn't have heard a peep. She's been sick in bed for two days. I've been waiting on her hand and foot."

"It must be going around," I said. "My aunt's sick in bed, too."

"What did they take?" June pivoted to survey the room. "I don't see anything missing." For a woman who was unwell, she seemed remarkably energetic.

"They took the cider donuts for Denny's birthday," Mr. Henderson said. "I came down this morning to let Xanadu out and saw they were gone."

"Is Xanadu a dog?" I asked. That might explain the missing donuts—or maybe they had a raccoon that liked to climb in through the kitchen window and take whatever he wanted.

Or I might be projecting.

"Xanadu's a cat, but she likes to go out in the mornings and soak up the sun," he replied.

June's hands slammed against her hips. "You called a P.I. over a box of donuts? What's wrong with you?"

"They're not just any donuts and now I've got to go out and find another gift for my brother," he said. "Besides, don't it bother you that someone crept into our house in the middle of the night and took something that belonged to us? What if they'd murdered us in our beds?"

"I haven't been in my bed so I suppose I'd be safe." Her gaze skated to me. "I've been staying in the guest room on account of being sick."

"She's considerate like that," Mr. Henderson said.

June smiled at her husband. "Don't want to get you sick, honey bun."

"Any sign of forced entry?" I asked.

"We don't lock our doors," June said. "This is a safe neighborhood."

"It *was* a safe neighborhood," Morty complained. "What am I supposed to do about my brother's party? I don't have the donuts."

"Who cares? You don't even like your brother," June shot back.

Morty crossed his arms. "Maybe not, but at least I'd get a good donut out of the deal. Goddess knows I deserve a reward for putting up with him."

I wasn't rested enough to endure their family squabbles. "Would you mind if I look around outside the house?"

Morty waved a hand. "Knock yourself out."

"I'll go with you," June said. "Xanadu needs to come inside and eat her breakfast."

June followed me to the front yard, calling the cat's name.

I scanned the ground for unusual prints. Maybe a hungry werewolf smelled the donuts during a nighttime run and took advantage of the unlocked door. Chances were low given that the full moon was on Monday, though. So far the only prints I saw belonged to the cat.

"You can stop looking," June said from behind me.

I spun around to face her. "You found something?"

"No, I mean you can stop because you won't find any evidence. I hid that box real good."

I stared at her. "You hid the donuts?"

"Right here." She patted her stomach with both hands. "I've been faking being sick for two days so I could take a vacation and read in bed. He's been feeding me nothing except vegetable soup and I'm starving. I snuck down in the middle of the night for food and saw those donuts." Her tongue swiped her lips. "I was so hungry that I pounced. Ate every last one in the box. No regrets."

"You should probably tell your husband."

"Are you nuts?" A cat shot past my leg and June scooped her up into her arms. "No way can I do that. Nobody holds a grudge like Morty. Plus he'll tell his brother and we already have bad blood between us on account of a drunken incident I'd rather not mention."

"June, your husband called the sheriff to investigate. Do you really think he's going to let this go without an answer?"

"Make one up then."

I really didn't want to insert myself in the middle of a domestic disagreement. I ran through a mental list of options until I settled on one.

"Where's the empty box?"

"I crushed it and stuffed it in the compost bin."

I wrinkled my nose. "I'm going to need you to get it." I drew the line at dumpster diving. Where was Raoul when I needed him?

She walked to the bin that stood against the side of the house and retrieved the box. Wiping off the food particles, she thrust the box at me. "Now what?"

"You go inside with the cat and distract him for a few minutes. Leave the rest to me."

June rounded the corner of the house with the cat in her arms and left me to work my magic.

Or Ivy's magic.

It was a crazy idea, but it might work. I sat on the lawn and focused on the empty box on my lap. I pictured Mr. Henderson holding the box with a dozen cider donuts nestled inside. I smelled the cinnamon and nutmeg in the batter. Magic thrashed inside me, begging for release. It seemed to sense what I was trying to achieve and was eager to help.

"Restituo," I said.

Magic pulsed through me and suddenly the box grew

heavier. The scent of cinnamon reached my nostrils. I looked down to see twelve donuts in the box. I gasped in disbelief. I couldn't believe the spell worked.

"Thanks, Ivy."

I picked up the box and carried it to the door where Mr. Henderson hovered just inside.

"Any sign of footprints?"

"No, but I did find these." I held up the box.

He gaped at the donuts. "Where on earth did you find those?"

June's jaw unhinged at the sight of the donuts.

"Outside on the roof of your truck," I lied. "Is there a chance you left them there and only thought you brought them inside?"

June set down the cat and joined her husband's side. "I bet that's exactly what happened, Morty. You've been so focused on me while I've been sick, you probably got mixed up."

"I don't know. I could've sworn I put them right there on the counter." He pointed.

June squeezed his bicep. "Sweetie, you probably just imagined them there."

Mr. Henderson seemed to take the suggestion under advisement. "I did forget to put the milk away after breakfast."

June lightly punched his arm. "There, you see? It was all a big misunderstanding. Now you let this nice lady get on with her day. I'm sure she has real crimes to solve."

That I did.

"I'm so sorry to bother you, ma'am," Mr. Henderson said.

"No problem. The sheriff would've been happy to help

you himself, but he's in the middle of a murder investigation."

"Oh, I read about that poor surfer," June commented. "I hope the sheriff finds who killed him real soon."

A memory of Zed's lifeless body flashed in my mind. "Me, too," I said.

I left the Henderson house feeling energized by the magic I'd performed. It was as though I'd been able to isolate a snapshot in time and bring it back into the present. I couldn't wait to tell Marigold the next time I saw her. If I could restore donuts that had been eaten, what else was I capable of?

I decided to pay a visit to Tony Alvarez at the old-fashioned barber shop on Cauldron Lane. As someone outside the immediate family circle, I figured Tony might be able to offer insight into Zed that his daughters were too blind to see.

He was in the midst of sweeping hair off the floor when I entered. Thick, dark curls covered his head. Toned biceps peeked out from beneath the short sleeves of a black T-shirt. His shredded jeans clung to muscular thighs.

Tina had good taste.

He glanced up from the floor. "The salon's down the street."

"I know. I'm looking for Tony Alvarez."

"That's me." He stopped sweeping and leaned on the broom handle. "What can I do for you?"

"My name's Ember Rose. I'm a private investigator."

His brow creased. "Ember Rose? Aren't you a reporter for *Vox Populi*?"

My breathing hitched. "I was. You read my articles?"

"Sure. What happened? You change careers or something?"

"Or something."

He set the broom against the wall. "That's too bad. You were good. The guy they got covering your beat now is a little too dry."

"Bentley Smith?"

He snapped his fingers. "That's the guy. You know him?"

"I do." I smiled, thinking of the elf whom I'd viewed as the brother I never wanted. I owed him a text.

Tony scrutinized me. "If you're a P.I., I'm going to go out on a limb and say you're here about Gina."

"I take it you heard the news about their father." If Tony was an avid reader of the local newspaper, he was bound to have read about the murder even if he didn't hear it directly from Tina's lips.

Tony raked his fingers through his curls. "Yeah, tough break. Zed was a quality dude." He gestured to one of the swivel chairs. "Have a seat, Ember Rose, former reporter. How'd you get caught up in their family drama?"

"Theirs? Aren't you family?"

He shook his head. "Not anymore. Glad to be out, too. They're a hot mess and I've got enough of my own issues. Don't need any of their baggage weighing me down."

"When did you get divorced?"

"Didn't. Never got married. Tina didn't believe in it. Said her parents didn't need a piece of paper to be happy together and neither did we."

"How did you feel about that?"

Tony shrugged. "I was upset at the time, but I guess it all worked out in the end, all things considered." He held up a hand and I noticed the shiny gold band on his ring finger.

"I never would've met the love of my life if I kept clinging to Tina. Annie's a great girl and, even better, she's an only child."

I thought of Aunt Hyacinth. "Isn't everybody's family a mess, though?"

"Not like them. The she-twins and their special brand of crazy." He exhaled. "When Tina's alone, she's terrific. Put her in a room with her sister and it's like a switch gets flipped that puts her in evil mode. I don't know how Gwen survived her childhood. The two of them against her would've been brutal. Gwen's too sweet."

"How would you describe your relationship with Zed?"

"Easy. Didn't have one. He kept everybody at arm's length. Even if I'd married Tina, I don't think it would've mattered. He didn't want to know me."

"Any particular reason?"

"He was pretty messed up after his partner died. That's Tina's mother. Stopped caring about anything. Never fully recovered either. I remember one time Tina and I had to drive over to Dusty Acres to convince the guy to shower. He stank like a sewer."

No wonder the house had fallen into disrepair. If Zed wasn't able to care for himself, he certainly wasn't capable of caring for a house. At least the condition of the bungalow showed signs that Zed's state of mind had improved since then. Maybe that was the reason he wanted to reclaim Dusty Acres. He felt ready to take ownership again.

"Do you recall hearing if Zed was in any kind of trouble?"

"Zed?" Tony made a dismissive noise. "Not so much as a parking ticket. He stayed home except to surf. One time I had to have a talk with him and he made me meet him at Balefire Beach at ten o'clock at night to have it." He chuckled at the memory. "For all his faults, Zed was a wonderfully weird dude. Starry Hollow lost a real character."

"Why did you need to talk to him?"

He waved a hand. "Oh, nothing important. Tina was worried about him. Said he seemed mad at her since he had to move out of Dusty Acres. She asked me if I'd check on him, so I made up a reason to see him."

"And you met him at the beach?"

"Sure did. Made me surf, too." He ran a hand across his face. "Let's just say surfing isn't my thing."

"Why agree to talk to him if you're not involved with Tina anymore?"

His cheeks turned red. "Tina's a hard habit to break, but I'm getting better at it. Annie helps. Anytime I start to forget Tina's bad points, I look over at my wife and remember what a heathy relationship looks like."

I understood the sentiment all too well. "Did Tina tell you what happened with Dusty Acres?"

"All I know is it ended up in the hands of one of my customers."

"Lou," I said.

He nodded. "I figure it had something to do with Gina."

"You didn't ask Tina about it when she sent you to talk to Zed?"

"That's not how it works. I ask too many questions and Tina stops talking. They're like a mob family that way." He shook his head. "Like I said, I'm glad to be out."

He didn't sound as 'out' as he seemed to think he was.

"Do you have any idea who might've wanted to hurt Zed?"

Tony tipped back his head. "Wish I knew. I don't like

the idea of somebody in this town whacking nice guys like Zed. It isn't fair."

"Murder often isn't."

The door blew open and an older man entered. His white hair stuck out in all directions.

"Hey, Mr. Curtis." Tony flicked his gaze to me. "Got a customer. Got any more questions or are we done?"

"We're done." I produced a business card and passed it to him. "Let me know if you think of anything else."

"Sure thing."

Mr. Curtis settled in the cushioned red seat. "Mrs. Curtis says I look like a shaggy dog from them movies in the 70's. She won't let me in the house until I've been to see you."

Tony winked at me. "Let's see if I can get your marriage back on track, Mr. Curtis."

If a haircut was the main bone of contention between them, the Curtises were doing pretty well.

I left the shop and headed for home.

Chapter Fifteen

I stopped by my office and was pleased to see Granger in the parking lot.

"I was going to call you as soon as I got inside," I told him.

He planted a kiss on my lips. "I'm so glad I can do that again." He tested his jaw. "Everything feels right as rain."

"Are you sure? You might want to test it one more time to be sure."

Grinning, he gripped me by the shoulders and planted another kiss on my mouth. This one sparked a small fire in my gut that was in danger of spreading to all my extremities.

"Anybody waiting for you in that office of yours?" he asked with a mischievous twinkle in his eye.

"Only a mountain of paperwork."

"How would you feel about wrinkling a few papers?"

I clasped his hand and practically dragged him toward the Sidhe Shed.

"Would you like the update on the investigation now or later?" I asked.

"During?"

"Very sexy."

We entered the shed and I quickly locked the door behind us. He grabbed me by the waist and kissed my neck.

"Have I mentioned how much I enjoy having your office right next to mine?"

"If the shed's a-rocking, don't come knocking," I joked.

He blazed a trail of kisses down the curve of my neck that curled my toes.

"I need to make up for lost time," he whispered.

"Don't make it up too quickly. Slow and steady wins the race."

"Don't you worry, Rose. By the time I'm done, we'll both be winners."

No lies detected.

Reluctantly I shooed him out so that he could get back to work and I could get home in time to cook dinner and get changed for this evening's coven ritual. I wasn't looking forward to the event, mainly because it was meant to be a mother-daughter bonding affair and I wasn't in the best headspace for it. I'd forgiven Marley for her error in judgment, but we remained at an impasse where Jinx was concerned. And, of course, Jinx would be present tonight along with her delightful mother.

Marley and I donned our official Silver Moon cloaks and tucked our wands in the deep recesses of our respective pockets.

"Do you think I should bring Ivy's wand instead?" Marley asked.

"Not for a coven ritual. It might draw unwanted attention." Even though I was now the receptacle of Ivy's magic, most members of the coven didn't know that. If they realized Marley was holding Ivy's wand, they might get skittish.

Deserved or not, my ancestor didn't have the best reputation.

We arrived at the designated clearing in the woods and Marley immediately spotted Jinx. She tugged my sleeve. "Can I go talk to her before it starts?"

"Of course," I said through gritted teeth. I didn't want to make a scene in front of the coven.

Across the clearing I spotted a friend of my own—someone I'd been meaning to talk to.

"Delphine Winter, just the witch I want to see."

The librarian smiled at me. "Good to see you, too, Ember."

"I have a question for you." I took her by the elbow and steered her to a secluded area among the live oaks.

"Ooh, we're out of earshot. This must be a very interesting question."

"It requires your librarian hat."

She pretended to place an invisible hat on her head. "Ready."

"Have you read about a situation where a witch merges with her magic?"

"Merges? I'm not sure what you mean. A witch performs magic. Magic isn't a living entity. Not in the strictest sense of the word."

"I know, but sometimes magic becomes so powerful that it controls the user, right? Doesn't that imply there could be a situation where you can no longer tell where the witch ends and the magic begins?"

The lines across her brow deepened. "This is a highly philosophical question, Ember."

I reached for the easy lie. "It's for a research paper Marley is writing for school."

Her features relaxed. "Oh. That explains it." She pulled

out her phone and tapped the screen. "There are a few treatises I can recommend. *Hawthorne on the Craft* is currently in stock. There's also the *Monroe Doctrine*. It's complex but thorough."

"What does the *Monroe Doctrine* have to do with magic?"

She looked up at me. "Not James Monroe. Flora. Unrelated as far as I know."

"Would you mind putting those books on hold for me?" I cleared my throat. "For Marley, I mean."

"Sure. They're not the most popular books in the library, so I don't think anyone will be fighting you for them."

The sound of a tinkling bell alerted us to the start of the ritual.

"We should get back," Delphine said.

We hurried to the clearing and I took my place beside Marley. My gaze briefly met Twila's. She didn't smile.

The feeling's mutual, lady, I thought.

Who are you looking at and why do you hate each other on an epic scale?

My gaze darted around the clearing. *Raoul? Where are you?*

In the tree above Hazel's head. I was thinking about dropping down in the middle of the ritual to liven things up a bit.

Please don't. Aunt Hyacinth wants us to make a good impression tonight.

On cue, my aunt appeared beside me. "Good evening, Ember."

"Glad to see you're feeling better."

"My throat is a bit scratchy, but I couldn't miss the ritual. It only happens once a year."

I waved to Aster and Linnea across the unlit bonfire.

"I hope you were able to prepare for tonight," my aunt said.

Prepare? Uh oh. "Of course," I said quickly. "I love a good unity ritual. Don't we, Marley?"

Marley nodded, uncertain what to say.

"Shouldn't you be standing with your children?" I prompted. "Looks like we're about to start."

"All in good time. The ritual doesn't start until I say so."

Leave it to my aunt to one-up the High Priestess. "Where is Iris?" I scanned the crowd for Iris Sandstone, the actual High Priestess.

"She's preparing the wine," Aunt Hyacinth said.

Right. The wine. I really should've boned up on this ritual before tonight. The last thing I wanted was to embarrass my aunt now that we were on good terms.

Iris unhooked her cloak and raised her hands in the air. "Welcome, sisters of the Silver Moon coven. Tonight we are here to reaffirm our bonds of love and unite as one."

I pictured a giant nesting doll filled with witches. Probably not what she meant by uniting as one.

"Each group will have the opportunity to demonstrate and deepen their familial bond."

Marley shot me an anxious look. I couldn't decide whether she was concerned with my performance or hers.

Probably mine.

"Maiden, Mother, and Crone," Iris intoned, "tonight we fortify the branches of our family tree. We heal our troubled hearts and grant forgiveness to those who require it."

Well, that was a timely message from the universe.

"The fire will rise as a show of your strengthening bond," Iris continued.

It reminded me of the carnival game where you use a

sledgehammer to see if you can make the bell ring. I wasn't any good at that game. Hopefully I'd be better at this one.

"Who would like to start us off?" Iris's gaze swept the circle. "Hyacinth?"

My aunt stepped forward, along with Linnea and Aster. They stood at three different points around the bonfire and raised their arms in unison. I took mental notes so I could copy them when our turn came.

"Strong and true is our bond," they chanted. "What once was broken is whole again."

Flames erupted from the bonfire like an active mini-volcano. I half expected the ground to tremble in response. The heat from the fire was hot even from this distance and I prayed they managed to keep their eyebrows intact.

"They're not even using wands," a voice whispered behind me.

"It's because there are three of them," someone else replied.

Hardly. It was because they were descendants of the One True Witch.

I was surprised when Twila and Jinx volunteered to go next. I wouldn't want to follow that performance.

Mother and daughter took their positions across the bonfire from each other and waited for the fire to reduce to embers before they began. They performed the same recitation, except instead of raising their hands above their heads, they aimed their wands at the bonfire. Jinx held hers beneath the sleeve of her cloak and I wondered whether she was trying to make it appear as though she didn't need one, like my aunt and cousins. Her expression crumpled when their fire only managed to burn about three feet high and with far less intensity.

"Can we try again?" Jinx asked, once the fire evaporated.

"Once is quite enough," her mother ground out.

Iris seemed to sense the tension and said, "I don't think one more time would do any harm."

Mother and daughter repeated their lines. This time when Jinx aimed her wand, a small puff of blame smoke emanated from the tip and Jinx fell backward on her bottom.

Twila's expression was so hard, her head could've been mounted on a statue. It seemed that their bonds had neither strengthened nor deepened tonight. I found myself feeling a little sorry for Jinx. The young witch scrambled to her feet, mumbling an apology. For a talented witch, I was surprised she fumbled her part so badly. I chalked it up to performance anxiety.

When it was our turn, I made sure to release a minimal amount of magic. I didn't want to risk burning down the forest. Then again, my relationship with Marley wasn't at full strength at the moment, so that fact would probably limit the damage I could do. We made a respectable showing, although I felt guilty that the ritual didn't completely wash away my complicated emotions.

"Everyone join hands around the bonfire," Iris instructed once each group had finished. "Be sure at least one of those hands belongs to a family member."

Marley and I clasped hands and stepped forward to join the circle.

"Now, repeat after me. Great Goddess of the Moon, hear us and reward our fealty. I reaffirm my bond to you," Iris said.

Marley and I turned to look at each other. "I reaffirm

my bond to you," we repeated, although neither of us seemed particularly enthusiastic about the idea. I wondered whether Jinx and Twila were having the same experience. Doubtful since Jinx seemed to have been a disappointment to her parents for years now whereas Marley's behavior was only recent.

Although I continued to hold Marley's hand in mine, we avoided eye contact. It seemed we were both too sincere to fake it for the crowd.

Iris lifted a large copper jug from the ground and held it aloft. "As a show of unity, we now drink from the same cup."

The High Priestess brought the jug to her lips and drank, then passed it to Calla beside her. I watched in horror as each witch drank from the same jug. There was a reason I owned a mug with the words 'no, you can't have a sip' emblazoned on it.

My pulse started to race. *It's headed this way.*

You want me to drop in now and run interference? Raoul asked. *I can knock it out of Marigold's hands before it reaches you.*

Everybody knew the raccoon was my familiar. They'd blame me for ruining the ritual.

Thanks, I'll suck it up.

Don't suck. Just sip.

Marley passed the jug to me and I pretended to sip before passing it to Aster. Problem solved—or avoided.

I was pleased to make it through the ritual without incident. Marley and I drove home in relative silence. The moment we got in the car, she'd stuck her earbuds in her ears and listened to music all the way to the cottage.

As we passed through the gate, I spotted a flying squirrel-shaped silhouette perched on the fencepost closest to the garden.

"You go ahead and get ready for bed," I told Marley. "I'll just be a minute."

I waltzed over to greet our gargoyle.

"Hey, Rocky. You look like you're holding a vigil out here."

The creature stared back at me with his enormous eyes.

"What we've got here is a failure to communicate," I said.

The flying squirrel gazed at me, unblinking.

"Not a *Cool Hand Luke* fan, huh?" An idea occurred to me. "You know what? I might be able to help with that. Not the *Cool Hand Luke* part, the communication part." I held up a finger. "Wait right here."

I wasn't sure how much he was able to understand, so I mimed the order too. I hurried into the cottage and went to the altar Raoul had made for me. I opened my grimoire and searched for a spell that could help me understand Rocky and vice-versa.

I smacked the page. "Bam. Got you."

While Marley showered upstairs, I gathered the materials. It wouldn't take long, assuming I performed the spell properly.

I mixed the ingredients in a glass jar and raced outside in the hope that Rocky was still holding court.

The flying squirrel remained still as I approached with the jar.

"Hey, Rocky. I've got a treat for you." I stuck the spoon in the mixture and offered it to him. It took a moment, but he finally stretched forward to sample the concoction.

"That tastes like your dirty gym socks," he said.

I broke into a smile. "Hey, it worked!"

"Is this what you wanted? An intimate conversation with the Leon?"

"Oh, your name is Leon?"

"*The* Leon."

"Nice to meet you. I'm..."

He rolled those big eyes. "I know who you are, cupcake. As you might have noticed, I've been staking out your house for days."

"And why is that?" I inclined my head. "There's something you want in the garden, isn't there?"

"Why don't you take down that ward and I'll show you?"

"Uh, no. I don't think so. Tell me what you want and maybe I can help you." I hated to admit it but Raoul was right. This flying squirrel had an attitude problem.

"Anybody ever tell you you're a pain in the rear end?"

"Many people, but they generally have to get to know me first."

"I'm a little quicker on the uptake."

I crossed my arms. "What's in this garden that you want? Because I can promise you right now, you won't get it without my help, which means you might want to be a smidge nicer."

He mimicked my voice.

"Listen, it's late and I'm tired. I thought I'd do you a favor since you've been so patient out here, but I can see you're not interested in my help."

"I can do this without help, lady."

"The fact that you're still sitting here four days later suggests otherwise."

Leon scampered down the fencepost and disappeared into the darkness.

Magic & Midnight

I stormed back to the cottage. I should've listened to Raoul and not wasted my time. He told me the squirrel was a jerk, but nooo. I had to override his actual experience with my 'big eyes' argument. When would I finally learn that looks could be deceiving?

Chapter Sixteen

I spent the next morning updating Granger on the investigation in my office. He brought the coffee. I brought the information.

He tapped the notepad. "Why'd you make a frowny face next to the note about the last time Gina saw her father?"

"Because she said he stopped by to say hi, which seems completely out of character."

"Why would she lie? It was two weeks ago. It isn't like she killed him right then and there."

"It's possible she was trying to hide a motive. I suspect he tried to talk to her about Dusty Acres. Maybe that's when he discovered she'd lost ownership."

"And when he decided to contact a lawyer."

I nodded. "I'm not sure why Zed's meeting with a lawyer would prompt her to kill him, though. Gary said Zed wanted to acquire property. He wasn't planning to go after Gina."

"People don't always behave rationally, Rose. You know

that." He tucked the notepad inside the file. "You've done a great job as usual, not that I expected anything less."

"Not great enough. The identity of the killer is still a mystery."

He grinned. "Yeah, but at least you solved the more pressing mystery of the missing donuts."

I tapped my pen on the table, thinking. "Is there anybody else you think we should talk to about Zed?"

He leaned back against the chair and sighed. "I spoke to the witnesses from the party yesterday, but no surprise they were too drunk to remember anything. Nobody could describe the noise they heard either, other than to say it was loud. Did Gina or Gwen mention any friends? Someone Zed spoke to regularly?"

"No. Gina said Zed's only real friends seemed to be the fish in the sea." I snapped my fingers. "You know what? That's not a bad idea."

His mouth quirked. "Last time I checked, fish weren't too chatty."

"No, but mermaids are. I bet you dollars to missing donuts that Zed was friendly with local merpeople." Zed was a fixture at the beach and he surfed at night when no one was around. It was only natural that he'd strike up a conversation with merpeople. Maybe one of them even witnessed something significant the night of the murder.

"You've done more than enough, Rose. I'll take it from here."

I gave him a pointed look. "How does a werewolf expect to interview merpeople? You know how twitchy you get in the water."

"I'm perfectly capable of conducting an interview with our water-based residents."

"How about this? You take Balefire Beach and I'll take the cove by The Lighthouse."

"Why the cove? Zed wasn't killed there."

"I know, but it's the mermaid hangout. If there's gossip to be shared, that's where they're sharing it."

"Up to you, Rose, but I don't want this to take up all your time. I'm sure you have your own stuff you need to focus on."

"It's a murder investigation, Granger. If that isn't a priority, then I don't know what is."

He gazed at me with affection. "There's that determined spirit I fell in love with. You want to drive over there now?"

"I have to hit the library after this. Delphine set aside a couple books for me. Then I'm having lunch with my cousins."

"You and I seem to have different definitions of the word priority," he teased.

"Hey! I'm definitely going to the cove today, but I think it makes sense to go at night. Merpeople are like everybody else when it comes to schedules. The ones who might've been around for Zed's midnight murder aren't going to be available at ten o'clock in the morning."

He wagged a finger at me. "Always thinking, Rose. In that case, I'll wait to go until later too. What's at the library? Getting cozy with great works of literature?"

I snorted. "I'll let you know after I've read them. They're nonfiction books about magic."

He pretended to snore. "I'll stick with Jack Kerouac." He rose to his feet. "I'll check in with you later and let you know if I learn anything new."

I smiled up at him. "I know I've said it before, but we really do make a great team."

The werewolf winked. "Don't tell Raoul. He might worry you're going to replace him."

"He's always worried I'm going to replace him. If not with you, then with a flying squirrel."

"Put yourself in his paws," Granger said. "He was alone before the two of you found each other. That probably comes with a lot of insecurities. Maybe he's afraid he'll lose you and be alone again."

Granger was right. It wouldn't surprise me to learn Raoul had abandonment issues.

"Good point. I'll have to think of a way to convince him he's stuck with me forever."

He leaned down and brushed his lips against mine. "Let me know what you come up with so I can do the same to you."

I cupped his cheek in the palm of my hand. "Mission already accomplished."

"Want me to drop you at the library? I'm going to pass right by."

"Thanks, but it's a nice day. I think I'll walk." It was the only way to squeeze in exercise today.

By the time I reached Delphine at the counter of the library, my forehead and armpits were sweaty and I could feel my hair frizzing with each step.

The witch took one look at me and gulped. "Did you run here?"

"You would think." I braced myself against the counter to recover. "I clearly need to make more of an effort to exercise." My body felt like it was careening toward eighty.

Delphine withdrew the books from the shelf behind her and set them on the counter. "I hope these help."

"Thanks. Did you put a slip in here with the date they're due back?" Otherwise I'd never remember.

Delphine smiled. "I'll send you a reminder text."

She knew me too well. "You're the best. How's everything with Wren?"

Her expression turned dreamy. "I couldn't ask for a better relationship."

"That's good to hear." I was very fond of both of them, so it was nice to know they were smitten with each other.

"How's everything with Sheriff Nash?"

I hugged the books to my chest. "I couldn't ask for a better relationship."

Delphine laughed. "Sounds like we both got lucky."

"I think they've done pretty well for themselves, too."

"I hear Florian and Honey are going strong."

I eyed the pretty witch. "You okay with that?" There was a time when I thought Delphine and Florian would go the distance, but not anymore.

"I'm really happy for him. For both of them." She sounded sincere.

"I wouldn't start planning their wedding yet, but they're off to a roaring start."

"They seem like a better match than Florian and I ever were."

As much as I adored Delphine, I didn't disagree.

I left the library and carried the books to Palmetto Inn where Aster and Linnea awaited me. Linnea had a lull between guests and had invited Aster and I for lunch. I wasn't one to turn down a free lunch.

"A little light reading, Ember?" Aster asked, when I put the books on the kitchen counter with a thud.

"Reference books from the library."

"For Marley?" Linnea asked.

"Not this time," I said vaguely. I didn't want to talk to

them about Ivy though. I was hungry and the smell of lasagna was making it difficult to focus on anything else.

"I hope you're hungry because I made enough for the whole coven," Linnea said, as though reading my mind. She pulled two pans of lasagna out of the oven. "One is veggie and one is meat."

I salivated at the sight of all the cheese. "And what are the two of you having?"

Aster popped the cork off a bottle of red wine and poured three glasses. "I hope nobody objects to a drink with lunch. I've been self-medicating this week."

"Still dealing with supply chain headaches?" I asked.

Nodding, she passed me a full glass of wine. "Sterling keeps telling me to be patient, but it's not my strong suit. You know I like to get things done."

Linnea cut three squares of lasagna and put them on plates. "It's such a beautiful day. Should we sit outside?"

"Sounds good to me." I carried my plate and wine glass to the back patio. "I heard a rumor there are wedding bells in your future, Linnea. Any news you'd like to share?"

Linnea straightened in her chair. "I heard the same rumor."

Aster gently kicked her sister's foot under the table. "And?"

Her fingers curled around the base of her glass. "And my guess is as good as yours. We've flirted with the idea but nothing concrete."

My New Jersey upbringing didn't let me beat around the bush. "Do you want to get married again?"

Linnea's cheeks were tinged with pink. "I don't know. My first experience wasn't so great."

"But you love him, right?" I asked.

"Of course, but sometimes love isn't enough." Linnea focused on the lasagna, cutting her piece into small squares.

"I think somebody has a case of ice cold feet," Aster said.

"Bryn and Hudson like him, don't they?" I pressed. "They wouldn't object to Rick as a stepfather."

"They adore him. He's more of a father figure than Wyatt. He helps me run Hudson to and from sports activities. He studies with Bryn." A smile passed her lips. "He's made a relatively seamless transition into our family."

"Speaking of family, everything okay with you and Marley?" Aster asked as we sat around the small table. "You seemed tense at the unity ritual."

I sighed. "We're having a teenager moment."

My cousins wore matching expressions of shock.

"Marley?" Linnea asked, aghast. "What happened?"

I told them about Jinx.

Linnea's head bobbed in solidarity. "Welcome to the teen years, full of external influences and attitude adjustments."

"I don't think it's limited to the teen years," Aster interjected. "There's a wizard at playgroup called Steven that showed Aspen how to bite the other children. I was mortified."

"That's because his name is Steven," I said. I remembered a Steven from elementary school that liked to eat chalk and a Steven from high school that liked to burn other students with cigarettes.

"Bryn and Hudson have both had friends I disapproved of," Linnea admitted. "The key was to let the friendship run its course. It inevitably did in both cases."

I savored the flavors of cherry and spices as I sipped the

wine. "I just hope it runs its course before anything too terrible happens."

"Hudson's friend was the worst," Linnea said. "A werewolf called Lucas who was constantly goading Hudson into daredevil behavior and Hudson couldn't set his ego aside to say no thanks. I was terrified he was going to end up taking after Wyatt."

"What ended it?" I asked, curious. I'd managed to devour every bite of lasagna on my plate and was secretly hoping for seconds.

"Hudson finally stopped acting like a performing monkey and Lucas stopped showing interest in him. It seems he didn't want a friend. He only wanted someone he could control. I was relieved it happened before Lucas persuaded him to do anything too dangerous."

It was reassuring to hear I wasn't the only one in an uncomfortable situation with my child. Even though I knew my experience wasn't unique, I'd felt alone until now. In fact, Linnea and Aster had never let me down. I knew I had to do a better job of letting them in.

"About those books," I began.

They snapped to attention. "Is this about the murder investigation?" Aster asked.

I didn't want to keep secrets from my family anymore, and certainly not from the ones I trusted.

"No. This is about Ivy Rose and her magic."

"Ivy?" Aster repeated. "Is Mother still giving you a hard time? I thought the two of you moved past that."

"We did. This isn't about your mom. It's about the magic itself, which is pretty potent in case you were wondering."

"Is that what the library books say?" Aster asked.

I downed the rest of the wine in the glass. It was now or never. "No, it's what I say from personal experience."

They exchanged baffled glances.

"I have Ivy's magic," I announced. "And I'm trying to figure out if a part of Ivy is still...attached to it."

Linnea squinted at me. "What does that mean? You *have* it?"

I thrust out my arms. "It's in these veins. Ivy's the Hulk to my Bruce Banner except I don't turn green or have rage issues."

"I don't know what any of that means," Aster said.

"Is that the real reason you and Mother had a falling out?" Linnea asked. "I thought it was because you found Ivy's Book of Shadows and refused to give it to her."

I was shocked that Florian had managed to keep the secret.

"She was angrier about the fact that I managed to access Ivy's magic. Ivy stored it in her Book of Shadows and I figured out how to unlock it."

Aster cast me a sidelong glance. "What a clever clogs you are."

Linnea examined me closely. "What does this mean for you? Your spells are more accurate? More powerful?"

"Yes and yes. I didn't mean to take the magic. It was an accident, but now that I have it, I need to learn how to control it."

Understanding registered in Aster's eyes. "Because you don't want to become the next Ivy."

I shook my head. "I have Marley to consider." And Granger. We were in a great place right now. It wasn't the time for magic meltdowns.

Aster sipped her wine. "So Ivy hid her magic in her Book of Shadows before they could strip the magic from her?" She paused to contemplate the enormity of the question. "Wow. Our ancestor was…"

"A badass," Linnea finished for her.

"But you think Ivy is somehow still connected to the magic?" Aster asked. "That doesn't make any sense."

"I know. That's why I'm doing research. I'm trying to understand why I sometimes feel a presence."

"Are you using her wand?" Aster asked.

"No, Marley had it, but I took it and put it in my closet with the grimoire and the Book of Shadows for safekeeping."

Linnea scraped off the cheese that was stuck to her plate and ate it. "Do you think they need to be kept safe even now?"

"I wouldn't keep Ivy's possessions all in one place," Aster advised. "There's a reason she kept them separate. I mean, she buried her Book of Shadows in the garden so no one would find it. That's excessive."

"That's because she was trying to keep the magic locked away. Now that it's no longer an issue, why does it matter?" I asked.

"Just because you unlocked the book doesn't mean those items are devoid of her energy," Aster explained.

I thought about my failed attempts to cleanse Ivy's wand of negative energy.

"What do you think I should do? Bury the book again?" Marley's herb garden was thriving. If I put the book back in the ground, I risked destroying the plants.

"I don't know that you need to resort to such extreme measures," Aster said. "Maybe just keep them in three different places. One in the cottage, one in your office, and the third…" She shrugged.

"Basically you want me to draw and quarter Ivy's magical objects," I said.

"Technically there are only three objects, so we're suggesting you third them," Linnea replied.

"I guess I could keep the wand at home, the grimoire in my office, and bury the Book of Shadows in the woods behind the cottage."

Aster nodded. "It makes sense to keep the book at bay. It's the most personal of the three."

"And where she stored the magic," I added. "I'll read through the library books and see what else I can learn."

Linnea reached for my hand. "We're here to help, Ember. Whatever you need."

Aster placed her hand on top of her sister's. "That's what family is for."

My chest constricted. Once again my cousins didn't disappoint. Whatever my aunt's flaws, I had to give her credit. She raised three pretty amazing children and I, for one, was grateful.

Chapter Seventeen

I returned to Rose Cottage and found Marley seated at the table with a bowl of sour cream potato chips. "Hey, Mom. Happy Friday."

"I didn't realize how late it was."

"I took PP3 for a walk when I got home."

"Thank you, sweetheart."

I went straight upstairs to retrieve the Book of Shadows before I forgot. I preferred to bury it in the woods while it was still light outside so that I could mark the spot for future reference, although I assumed the absence of growth there would offer a hint later on.

I entered the bedroom closet and immediately noticed the wooden box was open. Odd. I tried to remember the last time I accessed any of Ivy's possessions.

I peered inside and my heart skipped a beat. The grimoire and the Book of Shadows were present and accounted for but no wand. "Great Goddess of the Moon."

Raoul stood in the closet doorway. *What's wrong?*

I felt dizzy and pressed a hand against the wall to brace myself. "The wand is missing."

Why would you look in there for your wand?

I slammed the lid closed. "Not *my* wand. Ivy's."

The raccoon's dark eyes rounded. *That's not good. Do you think your aunt...?*

I shook my head emphatically. "No, we've moved past that. I'm sure of it." I paused, thinking. "What about your squirrel friend? Is it possible he found a way inside the cottage?"

Oh, now he's my friend? You keep telling me how cute and innocent he is. He tapped a claw on the doorjamb. *Maybe not so innocent now.*

But why would a flying squirrel care about a witch's wand? To destroy the ward around the garden?

My gaze drifted around the room and another memory slid into place, this time of a different interloper. Nausea gathered in my stomach.

"Marley!" Panicked, I burst from the bedroom to find my daughter.

She stood at the kitchen counter now, her head bobbing to music I couldn't hear.

"Marley," I shouted. I never shouted.

She froze, her gaze locked on mine. Slowly she removed an earbud. "What's wrong?"

The words nearly got stuck in my throat. "Ivy's wand is missing."

She wrinkled her nose. "How? I keep it under my mattress with my journal."

I grimaced. "Actually you don't. I sort of moved it a couple weeks ago. The wand, not the journal. I didn't read it either, I swear."

Her eyebrows drew together. "Why did you move the wand?"

"Because I wanted to keep Ivy's possessions in one place. I moved them all to a box in my closet." I drew a deep breath. "Did you tell Jinx about the wand? About Ivy?"

Her face hardened. "Seriously? You're going to try to pin this on Jinx? I'm the one who took the hat."

"I don't trust her, Marley."

Marley's face contorted. "What's your problem with her?"

"I caught her in my room snooping and now the wand is missing. Plus there was that incident at the ritual. You think it's a coincidence?"

Marley blinked. "You think she tried to use Ivy's wand at the ritual?"

Another memory surfaced. "She had it tucked up her sleeve. At first I thought she did that to make it seem like she didn't need one, but now I wonder if she was just hiding the wand she was using."

"That's ridiculous."

"Is it? Weren't you surprised when she couldn't manage a simple unity spell? She's supposed to be advanced. The wand probably rejected her."

Marley chewed her lip. "Even if she took it, I'm sure she didn't know what it was. She probably thinks she did you a favor by taking an old wand off your hands."

I gaped at her. "Marley, listen to yourself. You're making excuses for a thief and a liar." I didn't have time to argue with my daughter. Not now. The priority was the return of Ivy's wand.

I grabbed my purse from the counter and marched out of the kitchen.

"Where are you going?" Marley called.

"To see your friend and get the wand back."

Marley ran past me and blocked my path. "Mom, you're going to embarrass me. She'll never speak to me again."

"Good. You're better off without her."

"You hate that I found someone else. You want me to be little forever so you can be the only one I go to for advice. You're trying to control me just like Aunt Hyacinth tried to control you!"

I shook my head. "It isn't that, I swear. I'm thrilled that you made a friend. I want you to have friends and become independent, but if Jinx took that wand, then she's not the friend you think she is."

Marley folded her arms and glared at me. "Jinx didn't take anything. I'll go with you and prove it."

"Fine." I reached past her and opened the door. "Let's go."

We drove in silence to Jinx's house. I was too frightened to speak. If something happened to Jinx because of the wand, I would never forgive myself.

"Do we have to do this?" Marley asked as we approached the front door of the stately home. "I'm so embarrassed."

"There are worse things than embarrassment."

"She won't want to be my friend anymore. She'll be too mortified."

I ignored her and knocked on the dark red door. I was relieved when Jinx answered, looking alive and with all her limbs intact.

Jinx looked uncertain at our unexpected presence. "Hey, Marley."

"Hi, Jinx."

"Are your parents home?" I interrupted.

"No, they took my brother to a fencing match where he's sure to take last place. Why?"

"I believe you have something that belongs to us and we'd like it back."

Jinx laughed. "Why would I have something that belongs to you?"

"Because you took it from my bedroom the day I caught you in there," I said. "Don't deny it, Fern. We know you took a wand from us and we'd like it back."

Jinx scowled at the use of her given name and I wondered whether I looked that disgruntled whenever Aunt Hyacinth called me Yarrow.

She looked at Marley and I caught the look of disdain that flashed in her eyes.

"I don't know what you're talking about," Jinx said. "Why would I steal a wand from your crappy little cottage when I have my own?"

Confusion marred Marley's features. "You said Rose Cottage was charming."

"It's meant for a single dwarf. I don't know how you could live in a place that small. It's like living in your aunt's garage."

"Her garage is bigger," I said.

Marley's blue eyes filled with tears. "I don't understand."

"I do," I said. "Jinx played you. She pretended to be your friend until she got what she wanted."

"Why would you want an antique wand that belongs to our family?" Marley asked. "You're not a Rose."

"No, but with the right magic, maybe we can become just as powerful. Witches don't have to be descendants of the One True Witch or come from a long line of High Priestesses in order to be powerful."

It was the closest she came to admitting her deception.

"We need that wand, Jinx," I said. "It's too dangerous in inexperienced hands."

Jinx looked at me and scoffed. "Like it's safe in your hands? You lived most of your life without practicing. I heard you screwed up every lesson you ever had. That your tutors hated working with you."

"Maybe at first...but I improved." And my tutors became my friends. "But my skills are irrelevant. That wand doesn't belong to you."

"It belongs to me," Marley said in a quiet voice. She stared at Jinx with tears shining in her eyes. "You stole that wand from me."

"You think you deserve it?" Jinx snapped. "You didn't earn that wand. It was handed to you on a silver platter."

"And it's the only thing that ever was," I said. "Marley is a powerful witch in her own right. Even better, she's smart and compassionate and kind. And she would never betray a friend. Not for power. Not for money. Not for anything."

Jinx scowled. "I don't have the wand. Please leave before I call the sheriff's office."

I inclined my head. "Go ahead. Call. Maybe we'll have them search your house for the wand."

Jinx grew pale as she realized her threat could be used against her.

I held out my hand. "The wand, Jinx. Now."

Jinx withdrew the wand from the back of her waistband and aimed it at me. "I guess this is a good time to experiment again with it. Maybe the ritual was a fluke. External pressure, right?" Her gaze darted to Marley.

"What do you think you're doing?" Marley asked in a quiet voice.

"I'm going to wipe your mom's memory first and then

yours. When I'm finished you won't remember I have the wand. You won't even remember me, which takes care of my next problem. Now that I have the wand, I don't need to be friends with you anymore."

Marley pressed her lips together in an effort not to cry. "I thought you liked me."

"Good grief. Piano and homework and family dinners." Jinx pretended to snore. "You have to be the most boring witch I've ever met. And just for the record, Nolan was smiling at me that night in the shop, not you."

Marley gasped. "That isn't true."

"Of course it is. Why would he look at chopped liver when steak was right in front of him?"

As I stared down the barrel of the wand, I felt Ivy's magic rise up within me.

I raised my arms, preparing to conjure a freeze spell when Jinx blew backward. She hit her head on the wall as the wand clattered on the hardwood. Jinx dropped to the floor, moaning.

Marley and I exchanged glances.

"Did you do that?" I asked.

She shook her head. "It wasn't you?"

"I was getting ready, but I hadn't pulled the trigger."

Marley rushed forward to check on her former friend. "Jinx, are you okay?"

Jinx rubbed the back of her head. "Who are you? What are you doing in my house?" Her eyes narrowed. "Don't I know you from school?"

I scooped up the wand and tucked it in my back pocket. "We stopped by to see your parents, but apparently they're not home. You tripped on the stairs and hit your head."

"I can feel it. There's a lump."

Marley turned to me. "We should make sure she doesn't have a concussion."

"It's not a concussion," I said. "The spell she intended to do reverberated."

"I know, but she could still have one." She turned back to Jinx. "Stay awake until your parents get home."

"That's easy. They're due home in like fifteen minutes."

"I'll send Twila a text." I wiggled my fingers at Marley. "Let's go."

Jinx frowned. "Wait, I thought you were here to see them."

"We got what we came for," I told her.

"See you at school," Marley said.

Jinx climbed to her feet. "Yeah, whatever. I don't really talk to anybody in the lower grades."

So much for their BFF bracelet.

We left the house in a hurry. I sent a text to Twila to say that Jinx hit her head when I was there to pick up Marley, and that she seemed a little dazed and confused but otherwise okay.

"They're going to think the knock on the head made her forget me," Marley said as we drove home.

"That's for the best." The explanation would drag us into uncomfortable family dynamics that I didn't want to be part of. I'd only recently improved my own.

"What did she do wrong?" Marley asked.

I tapped my fingers on the steering wheel. "Where to begin? Befriending you under false pretenses was probably the first step. I guess she heard about Ivy's wand from somewhere." It didn't surprise me. Starry Hollow was awash in gossip, especially about a family as lauded as mine.

"I don't mean the whole plan. I mean the spell. Why did it backfire on her?"

"I have a theory, but I don't know for sure."

"Is it because the wand was Ivy's and you have Ivy's magic?"

I glanced at her, smiling. "Great minds think alike. The wand recognized its magic and triggered some kind of protective feature."

"Nobody can use Ivy's wand against you? That's pretty cool."

"Pretty lucky, you mean. Jinx could've made a real mess of our lives." And all for the sake of winning her parents' approval.

"I feel sorry for her," Marley whispered.

Leave it to Marley Rose to be completely bamboozled by a liar and a thief and still muster a healthy dose of compassion and empathy. My daughter taught me life lessons every day of the week and twice on Sundays.

"Her parents must be so hard on her to make her feel she had to take drastic measures," the Mayor of Compassionville continued.

I was inclined to agree. Jinx must've been desperate to impress her parents if she felt compelled to go to such great lengths, but it was Marley for whom I felt the most compassion. Jinx was perfectly content to march right over my daughter's feelings in an attempt to ease her own pain.

"Doesn't make it right," I said. "You don't deserve to be treated that way."

It wasn't until we parked in front of Rose Cottage that Marley burst into tears.

"I'm sorry, sweetheart," I said.

Bonkers must've sensed her distress because the winged kitten was waiting for her outside the cottage.

"I'm the one who's sorry. I should've listened to you," Marley whispered.

I pivoted in the seat to face her. "Then listen to me now. I want you to understand something—you are worthy of friendship. Not because you're a Rose. Not because you have access to powerful artifacts. Because you're Marley. You don't have to *earn* anybody's love or friendship."

She nodded emphatically as tears slid down her cheeks. I longed for the days when I could cradle her in my arms and comfort her on my lap.

"I love you, Mom. I'll never doubt you again."

"Don't say that. I want you to test boundaries. To question authority. To think for yourself. That's how you'll grow into the force of nature you were born to be." I kissed her forehead. "And I love you, too."

Marley opened the passenger door. "Aren't you coming in?"

"You go ahead. I have one more task I'd like to accomplish before bedtime."

"Now?"

"All this talk of friendship reminded me of something I need to do."

She lurched across the gearshift and kissed my cheek. "I'll see you in a bit."

"Do you want me to see if Florian is around to hang out with you while I'm gone?"

Marley pulled a face. "You think Florian's available on a Friday night? Don't worry. I can handle being alone."

"Why don't you call a friend?"

"I think I'm just going to write in my journal tonight. Maybe draw."

"Sounds like a plan."

I waited for Marley to enter the cottage before I drove away. My headlights picked up a familiar silhouette on the fencepost. I waved as I passed the flying squirrel and I was pretty sure he flipped me off inasmuch as a squirrel could mimic a middle finger.

I hoped I had better luck communicating with the merpeople. I'd interview a couple regulars and then head home for a good night's sleep. After the day I had, I deserved it.

Chapter Eighteen

The cove was dark and desolate when I arrived. With the moon obscured by clouds, the only light emanated from The Lighthouse nearby. I felt mildly disappointed. I was hoping to find a gaggle of mermaids on the rocks ready to dish the dirt. Now I'd have to flag one down and ask questions. I should've worn a swimsuit underneath my clothes.

I scanned the dark waters in search of a fin or ripples on the surface. The only waves were the ones rolling into the cove and crashing against the rocks. A soothing sound, but not the reason I was here.

I noticed a conch shell that had washed ashore and brought it to my lips. Somebody would respond to the noise. It was basically the Bat signal for merfolk.

Sure enough, I spotted the flap of a fin on the horizon. I waited patiently as a mermaid swam toward me. A head broke the surface and I recognized the tight brown curls of a mermaid named Bettina.

"Hey, Ember. Haven't seen you in ages. What brings you to the cove tonight?"

Magic & Midnight

"Where is everybody? Isn't there usually a group that hangs out here?"

"Not lately. Too much strange activity. Most of us are steering clear of the coast until things calm down."

"Then I'm probably barking up the wrong tree. I was hoping you might be able to help me with a murder investigation. Did you know the Midnight Surfer?"

"Of course. Everybody out here knows Zed. He's a wonderful man." Her expression crumpled. "Wait, you used the past tense."

"Zed was murdered on Sunday night on Balefire Beach." I was surprised Bettina hadn't heard the news, but if they were staying away from the coast, then it made sense they'd have missed out on the gossip.

The mermaid's mouth turned down at the corners. "That's too bad. He was as close to one of us as you could get without actual fins." Her own fin surfaced and she slapped the tail on the water to make her point.

"I was hoping one of you might have seen what happened to him the night he was killed. I'm all out of suspects and witnesses."

"If I had, I would've gotten word to that sexy sheriff. I'd take any chance to interact with that hunk of burning werewolf." She glanced down at her chest. "I'd wear my smaller shells. Show a little more skin."

I cleared my throat. "About the sexy sheriff…"

The mermaid stiffened as the sound of a motor interrupted us. I craned my neck to see the source of the noise. Unfortunately all I could see in the darkness were headlights.

When I turned back to Bettina, she was gone. "Bettina!" I tried the conch shell again, but no one answered the call.

The vehicle came to a stop and I noticed a second one

directly behind it. There wasn't much room for them in the cove. Technically they weren't supposed to be driving on the sand at all. I'd mentioned that to Granger when I tripped on the tire indentations at Balefire Beach.

The occupants of the vehicles didn't seem to notice me as they disembarked, which was unsurprising given the absence of light.

"This place is small," a muscular man said. "It'll only take a few hours tops."

"Better coverage, too," a second man said. This one's silhouette was tall and lanky. "Should've started here in the first place and saved ourselves a huge headache."

A third man emptied equipment from a pickup truck.

"I thought there might be mermaids here. Don't they hang out in the coves?" The muscular man turned to scan the water and noticed me. "Whoa. What are you doing here?"

"Visiting a mermaid friend," I said, "but your noisy motor scared her away."

The lanky man smacked the muscular one's arm. "Now you know why we haven't seen any."

"I can hardly control the noise level of the motor," the muscular guy replied. He shifted his focus back to me. "We've got a permit to deal with an erosion issue here. We're going to need you to clear out of the cove pronto."

I remembered a mention of the erosion issue at the Council of Elders meeting. "I'm glad you guys are here. Starry Hollow beaches have been suffering lately."

He gave me a curious look. "How so?"

"Climate change. What else?"

His shoulders relaxed slightly. "Yeah, it's a real problem."

I noticed the tool held by the third man. It looked like a

metal detector except for the bottom. With its slightly curved blade, it was shaped like a shovel.

I gestured to the tool. "What is that?"

"A power shovel," the third man said.

"Is everything motorized these days? What happened to good, old-fashioned manual labor?"

"A regular shovel's fine for a small job," the muscular man said, "but when you have a lot of sand to move and time is of the essence, you need more than muscle."

I frowned. "Is that how you fight erosion? You move the sand?"

"There's a little more to it than that," the lanky guy said. "It's too complicated to explain."

Wow. He was forgoing the opportunity to mansplain how they combat erosion? This guy was a rare breed.

"Any chance you were working at Balefire Beach on Sunday night?" The partygoers nearby had heard a loud noise. Maybe they'd heard this equipment.

All three men froze. The guilty expression on their faces made my veins turned to ice. The murder weapon was a slightly curved item capable of blunt force trauma.

I looked at the power shovel and the pieces fell into place. These men weren't fighting the effects of erosion. In fact, they were doing the exact opposite. They were fighting the effects of the supply chain issue.

"Why do you ask about Balefire Beach?" the tall and lanky man asked.

"Because I saw tire tracks in the sand on Sunday and was wondering if you might've been working over there."

Sand was a key ingredient in cement and my gut told me these men were mining sand for that very purpose. I'd bet Rose Cottage that these men were also responsible for stealing Oliver Dagwood's limestone materials. Limestone was also in short supply and a necessary ingredient to make—you guessed it—cement.

"We don't know anything about that," the muscular man said.

"Too bad. Anyway, it's late," I said. "I should let you guys get to work."

As I walked past them, I reached for my phone to send a text to Granger. He was probably at Balefire Beach right now trying to communicate with merpeople. Before I could type anything, the third man used the power shovel to hit my arm and knock the phone out of my hand.

"Oops," he said, smiling.

I kept my mask of innocence intact. "What was that for? I only wanted to call my daughter to let her know I'm on the way home."

I stooped to pick up the phone, but his boot blocked me.

"I don't think that'll be necessary, sweetheart."

A fourth figure emerged from the shadows. This one I recognized.

"Lou, we've got a problem," the muscular one said.

Lou Giordano stepped into the beam of light from the truck. "Hey, I know you. You came to the club to ask questions about Gina."

And I'd been so focused on Gina and Dusty Acres in my conversation with Lou that it didn't occur to me to look for another angle.

"She knows about the surfer, boss," the tall and lanky one said.

Lou didn't react. "She can't prove anything."

Maybe not, but I could at least get the answers I'd been seeking. "What happened? Zed stumbled upon your efforts to drain Balefire Beach of its sand?"

Lou shrugged. "Pretty much. We didn't expect anybody to be in the water at that hour."

"He wasn't happy when he figured out what we were up to," the muscular man said. "He tried to use his surfboard to destroy the equipment."

I crossed my arms. "So you killed him with the shovel and then staged it to make it look like a surfing accident."

"He was an old dude surfing in the dark," Lou said without an ounce of remorse. "Accidents happen."

Bile rose in my throat. "And why was his life worth less than a bunch of sand?"

He cracked his knuckles. "In case you missed it, there's a supply chain issue at the moment and it's destroying my construction business. My father will kill me if that happens. I need sand to make cement and keep things moving."

I waved a hand at the horizon. "There's a whole Sahara out there."

"Desert sand is no good for this," the tall and lanky guy interjected. "Beach sand is finer. We would've sucked up a nice chunk of Balefire Beach if the old hippie hadn't gotten in the way."

This must've been what Bettina meant when she referenced strange activity along the coast.

"Boss, what are we going to do with her?" the muscular one asked. "I don't mind the sand mining, but I didn't sign up to become no serial killer."

Lou hiked up his trousers. "It's either take care of her or get used to the inside of a prison cell. I don't know about you, but I get claustrophobic."

Muscular Guy at least had the decency to look conflicted.

I pushed up my sleeves. "I've got news for you. You're

not my first brush with a mobster." Granted, that experience nearly killed me, along with Marley and PP3. It was only thanks to the timely arrival of my Rose cousins that we survived the attack.

"I find the term mobster antiquated and offensive," Lou said.

"Where's the boat?" the muscular one asked. "We can put her body on it and dump her out at sea."

"It's not a boat; it's a dredging vessel," Lou shot back. "We don't have it tonight. The cove's too small."

A dredging vessel? An operation like this could wipe out all the sand in the cove in one night. No wonder Zed had confronted them. His love of the beach was too great to simply walk away and feign ignorance in order to save his own skin. I felt a stab of sympathy for the Midnight Surfer. The man may have been complex and crabby, but he died a hero.

"We can't bury her," the third man said. "There won't be enough sand left."

"We'll worry about the details later." Lou snatched the power shovel from his minion, clearly intending to whack me in the same manner as Zed.

Four men. One witch. Not my usual odds.

I dusted off the negative energy and tried to focus on the positive. *Confidence, Ember. You're the descendant of the One True Witch with access to Ivy's magic.*

I could do this. I had to.

I opened the valve and let the magic flow through me. It rushed through my extremities with torrential force but seemed to dissipate the moment it left my body.

Lou's expression softened and he lowered the shovel. "Before we whack her, I just want you guys to know I'm sorry I'm so critical of you all the time. It's only because I'm so critical of myself and I view you guys as an extension of me."

I balked. "Come again?"

"It's cool, Lou. We know you're doing your best," the muscular one said.

Wait. Which spell did I conjure?

"I lost ten pounds," the muscular one continued. "I was hoping somebody would notice, but I realize I'm proud of myself without the need for external emotional support. I'm finally learning to love myself and it feels good."

"You're a good person," the third man said. "We're all doing our best to survive."

Oh, wow. Now I understood. I'd accidentally cast the spell that banished negative self-talk.

"We still have to kill you," Lou explained, "but we won't beat ourselves up over it."

The muscular guy shrugged. "Yeah, it can't be helped."

The third guy scratched his cheek. "I don't know. I'm not sure I can look myself in the mirror if I kill a woman."

"And a mom," I added. "I have a daughter. Her dad's already dead so you'd be making her an orphan."

The third guy sucked the air between his teeth. "See, Lou? I'm trying to be the best version of myself here, but this ain't helping."

Time for a second attempt. I focused inwardly and sifted through my magic to find the right spell. Ivy had so many in her magical rolodex, it was hard to separate them.

A wave rolled toward us. The water rushed over our feet and receded. As the trio backed toward the vehicles, an idea took shape.

I tried to remember how I conjured elemental magic in the past. It was usually the result of extreme emotional pressure. But I reminded myself that was the old me. With Ivy in the mix, extreme emotional pressure should no longer be necessary.

I concentrated on the ocean lapping against the shore. I felt a connection to the water click into place.

"Venio," I commanded.

A second wave followed, this one bigger and stronger. The force knocked the third guy off his feet.

"What's going on?" Lou demanded. "Why is this happening?"

"Don't you remember, Lou? I'm a witch." I summoned another wave toward us. This one reached the tires of the vehicles and claimed the power tools.

"You're destroying our equipment," Lou thundered. "Do you have any idea how expensive all this is?"

"Bill me," I said.

The third guy struggled to his feet and started to run. Water splashed in all directions as he trudged to escape the waves. Finally he gave up and climbed into the flatbed of the truck.

As Muscular Guy tried to grab my arm, another wave crashed into the cove and knocked him off his feet. He immediately popped up, sputtering water. Lou was in the process of swimming toward the floating truck. The fourth guy was hanging from the bumper and kicking.

"Somebody stop her," Lou yelled.

"With what, a seashell?" Muscular Guy shouted.

Water swirled around my calves as the last wave receded.

"Looks like you need a lift."

I twisted toward the ocean to see Bettina. "I do. Thanks."

"Balefire Beach?"

"That works."

Magic & Midnight

She angled her head. "Should I get help for them? I have a few friends nearby."

I turned to see all four men now seated in the floating truck's flatbed. "I'll call for help when we get to shore. They'll be fine until then."

I hooked my arms around her neck and held on. I waved to my attackers as the water embraced us.

The mermaid craned her neck to talk to me. "You summoned all those waves, huh?"

"How did you know?"

"I felt drawn by the power and it guided me back to you. I recognize that magic, you know."

"Recognize it?"

Bettina glided to the shore on the crest of a wave and delivered me safely to the sand. "It belonged to the High Priestess."

I stared at her. "How old are you?" Bettina didn't look a day over thirty.

The mermaid offered a coy smile. "There are beings in the ocean much older than I. It's unexplored territory for you witches."

"And you recognized Ivy's magic? How is that possible?"

Bettina flicked her tail in and out of the water. "Magic has its own energy signature. I think it travels more clearly underwater."

There was no sign of Granger on the beach. I pulled my phone from my pocket and was relieved to see it wasn't drenched in salt water. I shook off the random droplets and texted Granger the location of his murderer and the accomplices.

"I think those men have been messing with our

ecosystem for weeks," Bettina continued. "I'm glad someone finally put a stop to them."

"Not blaming the victims, but if there was an issue, why didn't one of you complain to the Council of Elders? Or to someone who could help? You may not reside on land, but you're still part of this community."

Bettina examined me. "You make a good point."

"You should petition the Council of Elders to add a seat for a water-based paranormal. You deserve representation in this town."

She lifted her chin. "You're darn right we do."

"The next time there's an issue, I want you to contact me. I live at Rose Cottage right behind an estate called Thornhold. I can't promise miracles, but I have connections. Maybe I'll be able to help."

"Thank you, Ember. I will." The mermaid turned and dove into the waves, disappearing from view.

I wiped my hands on my hips and trudged through the sand toward home. I managed to retrieve Ivy's wand, reconcile with my daughter, wrangle a killer, thwart illegal sand mining activities, and embrace an underwater community—all in a day's work.

It was good to be a witch.

Chapter Nineteen

I stuck the broomstick in the middle of the herb garden and admired my handiwork. The glass eyes of the Franken-Beanie Boo stared in the distance. It was a toy black cat with soft bat wings sewn on—the closest we could get to mounting Bonkers on a spike to scare away Rocky.

"He's watching us from the woods." Marley pointed to the edge of the woods at the back of the cottage. "He's on that low tree branch."

I observed our stalker. "The fencepost is pretty low, too, isn't it?" The gears of my mind started clicking.

"What if he just stalks the perimeter for the rest of our lives, watching for an opportunity to swoop in?" Marley asked.

"That won't happen."

"How can you be sure?"

"Because I think I figured out what he wants and I'm going to give it to him."

Marley's brow creased. "What is it?"

"What's the plant primarily associated with the levitation of witches' broomsticks?"

Frowning, Marley looked at the contents of the garden. "Belladonna. But why would a flying squirrel need belladonna?"

"Think about it. We haven't once seen him actually fly. We've seen him in places where he was able to climb, yes, but we haven't actually seen him airborne."

Her mouth formed a small 'o.' "I can't believe I didn't think of that."

"You've been distracted."

Her gaze lowered to the ground. "I'm so sorry, Mom."

"No more apologies. We're good."

Her blue eyes shone with relief. "I don't ever want to be estranged like Zed and his daughters."

"Relationships take work. That includes the ones you have with family members." We could be as close as conjoined twins now, but if we didn't put the effort in to be good to each other, the relationship could erode just like Balefire Beach.

Of course, that one had a little extra help.

"Maybe we should call him over."

"He won't come now that we've put FrankenBonkers in the garden." Marley cut a glance at our creation. "If you give Rocky what he wants, will we need to keep the scarecrow? I hope so because he's kind of cute."

"I think it's a good idea. Even with the ward in place, we don't know what else this garden will attract in the future." It seemed to emanate more magic than we realized.

I strolled toward the woods with Marley beside me. "Hey, Rocky. I've got a present for you."

The flying squirrel scrambled down the trunk to the lowest branch. His eyes were their usual size of baseballs.

I held out the belladonna in the palm of my hand. "You should've told me why you needed this when I spelled you to talk." It just proved that talking didn't necessarily result in communication.

"He was probably embarrassed," Marley said. "A flying squirrel that can't fly."

Even the flying squirrel had an ego. That likely explained his attitude problem as well. He felt defensive about his inability to do something that should've come naturally. I didn't blame the little guy.

"I can't give this to you as is because it's poisonous," I told him, "but I can make a remedy for you. Meet me at the front of the cottage in an hour."

Rocky's head jerked back and forth quickly and he scampered away.

"Do you think we'll ever see him again after you give him the remedy?" Marley asked.

"Doubt it. He didn't want to be here, especially with his nemesis nearby." I motioned to the sky where Bonkers was coming in for a landing.

Marley tapped her shoulder and her familiar glided to rest there.

"I need to head over to Thornhold later. Want to come?"

"No, thanks. I have to study." She looked at me with solemn eyes. "I mean really study."

I offered a reassuring smile. "I believe you."

"Why do you have to go?"

"Because Aunt Hyacinth has questions about my report from the Council of Elders meeting. Apparently it wasn't detailed enough for her liking and she'd like to see me in person to fill in the gaps."

"Of course she does." Marley tickled Bonkers as we headed back to the cottage.

While Marley focused on schoolwork, I read through the relevant pages of the library books from Delphine. One option was to try to put the genie back in the bottle—direct Ivy's magic back to a receptacle where I could safely store it. In light of Jinx's actions, this wasn't my preferred option given that it left the magic vulnerable to theft by others. I paused when I reached the section about breaking down magic into its most basic components. If I could somehow break down Ivy's magic and disperse it, then I wouldn't have to worry about controlling it before it controls me. The magic would cease to have the same level of potency. I didn't see anything about a witch herself being attached to her magic after death. I continued to read until my eyes glazed over.

A furry paw slammed the book closed. *I think you've reached your educational quota for the day.*

"Hey, Raoul."

You look a little green around the gills.

"I probably overdosed on knowledge."

Too much knowledge makes me feel nauseated too.

"On the plus side, it did give me an idea. Up for a little field trip to the beach before I go to see Aunt Hyacinth?"

Me? Are you sure you don't want to invite one of your other companions? Maybe your special buddy the big-eyed squirrel?

I gave the raccoon a long look. "You're my familiar, aren't you?"

He slid down to the floor and saluted me. *Familiar Raoul reporting for duty, ma'am.*

With Raoul by my side, I headed to the beach toting a bag chock full of magical objects. I wasn't sure whether my idea would work, but it was worth a shot. Might as well put Ivy's powerful magic to the test and see what kind of good it could do in the world. I owed it to Zed and I owed it to Starry Hollow.

I trudged across the sand until I reached a spot close to the surf. I couldn't spread a blanket in case it muffled the spell so I planted my butt directly on the sand and placed a candle in front of me. Thankfully there was no breeze to blow out the flame or sand in my face.

I shifted to a cross-legged position and cleared my mind. Listening to the sound of the waves crashing against the shore helped. It was one of the most soothing noises in the world.

I concentrated on the grains of sand and tried to picture more of them—a snapshot in time before the thieves got their equipment involved. Magic rolled through me like the waves I now observed.

"Restituo," I said.

The sands shifted. Was it my imagination or did the beach seem...plumper?

Raoul's voice cut into my thoughts. *It worked.*

Elation flooded my body. I'd managed to access Ivy's powerful magic again and it hadn't taken control of me. I didn't want to give myself too much credit. A donut spell and a sand spell were hardly big battles, although admittedly the sand spell took a lot more magic than conjuring a box of donuts.

Raoul gazed at me in wonder. *You did it.*

Couldn't have done it without you.

Raoul grunted. *Pretty sure all I did was eat the snacks you packed.*

"That was helpful. It makes the bag lighter for the walk

home." I rubbed my hands together. "But first let's perform our little ritual."

Ours?

I dumped the rest of the contents from my bag and created a small bonfire on the beach.

"You and I are going to reaffirm our family bond."

The raccoon's mouth opened. *Like the unity ritual?*

"Exactly. Witches and familiars have one of the strongest bonds in existence. It deserves attention every now and again, don't you think?"

He dropped onto his plump bottom and settled on the sand across the bonfire from me.

I took his paws in my hands. "Repeat after me. Great Goddess of the Moon, hear us and reward our fealty. I reaffirm my bond to you."

Great Goddess of the Moon. Hear us and reward our fealty. I reaffirm my bond to you. He released my hands and searched the objects on the beach. *Where's the wine?*

I pulled two juice boxes from the bag. I poked a straw through the hole and set the juice box in front of the raccoon. "Drink."

His fixed his beady eyes on the box. *Could you at least spike it?*

I sucked the juice through the straw without answering.

After finishing our juice in celebration of our bond, we gathered our belongings and vacated the beach.

"I'm going to stop in and see Aunt Hyacinth," I said when we reached Thornhold. "I assume you don't want to join me."

Hard pass. I make it my mission in life to avoid that cat of hers.

Raoul and I parted ways outside Thornhold. I tracked down my aunt in her office.

Magic & Midnight

"Ember, are you ready to go through your notes?"

I dropped into the chair across from her. "First, I have a proposal of my own. I've been thinking it might be nice to mix things up on Sunday. Maybe throw a potluck dinner."

My aunt frowned. "Potluck?" She pronounced the word as though it caused her great discomfort.

"I thought we could have a theme, like Memphis BBQ or Taco Sunday."

"Are you dissatisfied with our usual fare?"

"No, not at all, but you always do the work—well, your kitchen staff does the work. I thought it might be a nice change if we all bring a dish."

Aunt Hyacinth gave me her full attention. "What prompted this?"

I didn't dare mention the pack picnic. My aunt would say no as a reflex if she knew I'd taken the idea from werewolves.

"It's something we used to do in New Jersey. I thought I'd bring a little hometown flavor to Starry Hollow."

She pondered the suggestion for a full minute. Finally she said, "I'll allow it this week as an experiment."

I slapped the arms of the chair. "Terrific. I'll bring the crescent rolls."

"What theme is that?"

"Oh, that's the theme I like to call I Love Carbs."

Simon knocked politely and entered the office.

"What is it, Simon?"

"Sheriff Nash is here to see you."

I twisted in my chair to observe him. "Me?"

"No, miss. He specifically asked for the lady of the house."

I frowned. "Did he get a flat tire on the way to the cottage or something?"

"Nope. All four tires are fully inflated." Granger emerged from behind Simon.

"Granger, what are you doing here?" I asked.

"I have business with your aunt."

"Since when?"

He swaggered into the office with an air of authority that I had to admit was pretty darn appealing.

Aunt Hyacinth took her sweet time dragging her gaze to meet his. "Have a seat, Sheriff."

"That won't be necessary. This'll only take a moment." He adjusted his sleeves. "Here's the situation. I'm in love with your niece and she's in love with me."

"Congratulations," my aunt said, unsmiling.

"And I think you should know that I plan to marry her."

"You do?" my aunt and I asked in unison.

Granger pivoted to face me. "This shouldn't come as a surprise to you. If it does, we've got bigger problems than your aunt's disapproval."

My aunt slotted her fingers together. "Is this your special way of asking for my blessing?"

"For the record, I don't care whether you disapprove, but I won't let you make our lives difficult solely because we didn't bow to your demands. Ember's been through enough and she deserves all the happiness in the world."

"I agree," my aunt said.

I jerked toward her. "You do?"

She kept her focus on Granger. "I don't disapprove, Sheriff. In fact, let me know when you're ready to pop the question. I'll volunteer to throw the reception. I have a certain amount set aside. I feel confident it'll meet your needs."

Granger's mouth open and closed. He seemed uncertain how to respond.

I smiled at him. "See? New leaf."

Aunt Hyacinth nodded. "New leaf. Gold, of course."

I shrugged. "New leaf. Same tree."

Granger hovered by the desk. Her unexpected acceptance appeared to take the wind out of his sails. He shoved his hands in his pockets.

"Well, good. I'm glad we're clear on that," he said.

"Would you like to join us for dinner on Sunday?" my aunt asked. "I know you're busy and I'd hate to deprive you of quality time with my niece. It's apparently a potluck designed around carbohydrates."

Granger stumbled over his response. "I...Sure, I'd appreciate that."

"Just so you know, there's a dress code."

"Suit and tie?"

"No, but if it's an outfit you'd find in your brother's wardrobe, don't wear it."

Granger chuckled. "I'll keep it in mind."

I reached over to clasp his hand. "About that proposal, will you give me advanced warning? I don't want to turn up in unicorn pajamas and unwashed hair."

"You might try simply not wearing juvenile sleepwear and ignoring basic hygiene," my aunt offered.

"I'm a working mom. That's completely unrealistic."

Granger rocked on his heels. "Now that that's settled, are you finished here, Rose?"

I cut a glance at my aunt.

"We can postpone," she said. "You seem to have more important matters to attend to."

"Great. Then how about I escort you home?" Granger asked. "It's Saturday night and I think that should involve a pizza box with our names on it."

"Pepperoni?" I asked hopefully.

"Ladies' choice."
I beamed. "I'd like that very much."

* * *

Be sure not to miss **Magic & Mirrors**, book 17 in the series.

Join my VIP List at www.annabelchase.com to receive FREE bonus content, as well as information on sales and new releases.

Printed in Great Britain
by Amazon